An Imprint of Ha

# *DEADLY STRANGER*

There was a loud thump from the front of the car. Startled, Kelly dropped the map and saw Lauren leaning against the hood of the car. She was facing the gas station, holding herself up with a hand on the hood of the Mustang. Her normally tan skin was grey as stone. Beyond her, the door to the gas station swung slowly closed on its spring hinges.

Kelly pushed open her door. "Lauren? Lauren, are you okay?"

There was a crash from the gas station as the front door flew open. Marshall stepped out into the sunlight. His face was as calm as ever, but his blue eyes were blazing. "What are you two doing back here?" he said in a cold voice.

*More heart-stopping Nightmares...*

# NIGHTMARES

# DEADLY STRANGER

## M.C. Sumner

Lions
*An Imprint of HarperCollinsPublishers*

First published in the USA in 1993 by
HarperCollins Publishers Inc.
First published in Great Britain in Lions in 1993
3 5 7 9 10 8 6 4

Lions is an imprint of HarperCollins Children's Books,
a division of HarperCollins Publishers Ltd, 77-85 Fulham
Palace Road, Hammersmith, London W6 8JB

ISBN 0 00 674757 4

The author asserts the moral right to be identified as the
author of the work.

Printed and bound in Great Britain
by HarperCollins Book Manufacturing Ltd, Glasgow

For my wife, who put up with me
quitting my day job; the members of the
Alternate Historians, without whom I
never would have sold a thing; and for
Sherwood, who gave me a boost when I
needed it.

# ONE

Kelly Tallon came awake at the first note of music from the clock radio. She smiled to herself. Her parents had been convinced that she wouldn't get up this early on the first day of spring break. But her parents had never understood Kelly's obsession with skiing. For a week of spring skiing in Colorado, she would have gotten up at four in the morning every day for a year.

Fumbling in the dark, she found the switch and managed to shut off the alarm. Across the room, her younger sister Amanda muttered something in her sleep, and the springs of her bed squeaked as she rolled over.

Kelly climbed out of bed. The hardwood floor was cool under her bare feet. She navigated

1

through the darkness until her hands found the clothes she had left on a chair. She peeled her nightshirt over her head and tossed it onto the bed, slid into her jeans, and pulled on a cotton sweatshirt.

She stepped carefully across the room toward the dresser. Her searching fingers picked out a brush in the pile of objects that covered the dresser's top. Squinting at the mirror above the dresser, Kelly ran the brush through her chin-length auburn hair. She wished she could turn on the lights.

*One more summer*, she thought. *I just have to get through this summer and I'll be out on my own.* College was only months away, and Kelly was anxious to get out of her house, out of high school—on with her life. She smiled, and she could just see the reflection of her white teeth in the darkened mirror.

She found her soft-sided suitcase where she'd left it by the door and hefted it with her left hand. The bag was heavy, filled with a week's worth of clothes. Kelly leaned far to the right as she opened the door and staggered into the hall-way.

Her skis and ski poles were waiting at the top of the stairs. The skis were several inches longer than Kelly was tall. Getting them balanced across her right shoulder was quite a trick. The combination of heavy bag and lengthy skis made her wobble as she walked down the hallway, the tips of her skis drawing figure eights in the air.

As she turned to go down the stairs, the skis cracked loudly against the wall. Kelly cringed. She stopped, waiting to see if there was any reaction. When no one stirred, she started down again. Two steps later, the skis hit the wall a second time. After that, Kelly took the steps very, very slowly.

She had to put her bag down to get the front door open. Stepping out into the cool morning air, she pulled her bag through and carefully eased the door shut behind her. Stars still shone overhead, but the sky in the east was turning gray-pink. A quarter moon floated between wispy clouds and reflected silver light from a yard covered in dew. Kelly walked across the grass, leaving dark footprints behind her. She sat her suitcase down by the curb and waited.

She didn't have to wait long. There was a screech of tires from the corner, and headlights spilled down the empty street. A blue Mustang, looking black in the moonlight, came sliding around the corner, sped down the street, and stopped in front of Kelly's house with a final squeal of burning rubber. Lauren Miki threw her door open and stepped onto the road.

"Morning," Kelly said cheerfully.

"It's not morning—the sun's not even up,"
Lauren replied. She arched her back and
stretched. "Come on, Kel. Let's get your skis
loaded."

Kelly had not taken two steps toward Lauren
before her mouth dropped open in surprise.
"Lauren! What happened to your hair?"

Lauren reached a hand up to the nape of her
neck and ran a finger across the bare skin. Her
black hair was cut short in the back and on the
sides, with thick bangs left to tumble across her
forehead. "What do you think?" she asked.

Kelly tilted her head to one side and studied
her friend for a moment. "It suits you," she said
at last. "It really shows off your face. But it's a bit
of a shock. You've had long hair since the second grade."

"Yeah, well, it's time to make some changes."

Lauren stepped onto the grass and took the
skis from Kelly. Almost a foot taller than Kelly,
Lauren handled the long skis with ease. She slid
them under an arrangement of cords and straps
that crisscrossed the Mustang's roof.

"Are you sure that rig is going to work?"
Kelly asked skeptically.

"Absolutely. I've got my skis in it too."

"All right. Just as long as my skis don't end
up on the interstate somewhere in Kansas."

Lauren popped the hatch open and tossed in

4

Kelly's bag. Packed together with Lauren's luggage, it made for a tight fit, and it took Lauren two tries to get the cover closed. As it finally clicked shut, a light came on in the upper floor of Kelly's house.

"Let's get going," Lauren said softly.

Kelly opened her door and started to get in, but another light came on in the house. She climbed back out of the car.

Lauren was fumbling for her keys. "Where are you going?" she asked, and Kelly was surprised at the tension in her voice.

"It's probably just my dad. I'm sure he just—"

"Get in," Lauren hissed.

"But . . ."

"Get in!"

She said it with such authority that Kelly didn't even think about arguing. She dropped into her seat and slammed the door. A moment later Lauren found the right key and ground the Mustang's motor to life. They shot off down the street just as the outside light of Kelly's house snapped on.

Looking back, Kelly could see a figure coming out her front door. "What was that all about?"

"What was what all about?" Lauren asked. She had a habit of evading questions by repeating them—a habit that always drove Kelly nuts.

"Why were you in such a hurry to leave?" Kelly said. "I'm sure my dad just wanted to give me his 'Be careful' speech."

"Maybe," Lauren said. She shifted the Mustang through its gears and made the turn at the corner so fast that Kelly was thrown up against her door. The back tires lost their grip on the blacktop, and the car began to spin wildly. Then Lauren fought it under control.

"Are you trying to get us killed, Lauren?" Kelly asked, her fingers tightly gripping her seat. "What's going on?"

"I didn't want you to talk to your dad, because your dad probably got a call from my dad," Lauren said. A traffic light turned red ahead of them, and Kelly was grateful that Lauren brought the car to a stop.

"So what was your dad going to say?"

Lauren looked over at her. Even in the dim light, her dark-brown eyes were bright. "That I don't have permission to go on this trip."

For the second time that morning, Kelly felt her mouth drop open. "Lauren! Why would he say that? I was there when he gave you permission. We've been planning this for months."

A car honked behind them, and they both looked up to see that the light had turned green. Lauren accelerated into the intersection. "It's my grades," she said.

6

"You've got great grades. When's the last time you made below a B?"

"Not my regular grades, my grades on the SATs."

Kelly frowned. "But I thought you did fine on those."

"Fine is not fine enough, my dear," Lauren replied, putting on a snooty accent. "Not if one expects to attend college within the selective ranks of the Ivy League."

"Now I'm really confused. I thought you were going to UCLA."

"Yeah, that's where I want to go. But of course, where I want to go doesn't count for anything." Lauren steered the car across the highway and onto the access ramp to the interstate. Even this early on a Saturday, the interstate was half choked with trucks and cars. Behind them the sun peeked over the horizon, and orange light shone across the highway, flashing from glass and chrome.

Kelly watched Lauren as she moved the car from lane to lane. She had always envied Lauren's beauty and maturity. Her height and figure had let Lauren pass for a college student before she was old enough to drive. Kelly hadn't grown an inch since she was twelve, and even at eighteen people still mistook her for an eighth grader.

Where Lauren had never had any shortage of boyfriends, Kelly's dates had been few and far between. While Kelly went through high school almost unnoticed, Lauren had been on several sports teams, a class officer almost every year, and a leader in more clubs than Kelly could count.

And then there was the money. Kelly's family wasn't exactly poor; they had a nice house and all the standard stuff. But Lauren's family had a huge house, and Lauren always had a new car and fancy clothes. Lauren was rich.

It was easy to be jealous of Lauren, but there was one thing that Kelly had never envied: Lauren's father. In all the times she'd met Mr. Miki, Kelly didn't think she'd ever seen him smile. No matter what Lauren did, it never seemed good enough for him. When Lauren got an A, he wanted it to be an A plus. When Lauren made cheerleader, he wanted her to be head cheerleader. When Lauren was on the volleyball team, he wanted her to be the star of the team.

"What are we going to do now?" Kelly asked.

"What do you mean?"

"Well, we can't go all the way to Colorado without permission."

"Why not?" Lauren said. There was a tone in her voice that made Kelly nervous.

"For one thing, we'll get killed when we get home."

Lauren gave a choked laugh. "My dad's already as mad as he's going to get."

"Yeah, but my dad's not that mad yet," Kelly said.

"Don't tell him."

Kelly frowned. "Don't tell him what?"

"Don't tell him you knew I wasn't supposed to go." Lauren paused to slide the car across two lanes and slammed on the gas to get around a line of slower-moving traffic. "He can't get mad at you if you didn't know you were doing anything wrong."

Kelly thought about it for a moment, then shook her head. "Won't work. As soon as we get there, I'm supposed to call in. And as soon as I do, my dad will tell me to beat it back home."

"What if you don't call?" Lauren suggested.

"If I don't, he'll probably have the National Guard after us. He made me promise to call every day."

"We could tell him the phone wasn't working."

"That might work for the first night," Kelly said. "But then what?"

Lauren slapped her hands against the steering wheel. "I don't know!" She closed her eyes, and Kelly fought the temptation to grab the wheel. But the car stayed straight until Lauren opened her eyes again. "I don't know," she repeated more softly, "but I'll figure out something by the time we get there."

Kelly put a hand on her friend's arm. "I think this is a bad idea, Lauren. You know how much I wanted to go on this trip, but I think the best thing we can do is go home. Maybe if we talk to your dad, he'll change his mind."

"He won't change his mind," Lauren insisted. Her dark eyes were fixed on the road ahead. "I'm going."

"Lauren . . ."

"No. If you want me to take you back home, I will. But I'm going."

Kelly bit her lip and tried to figure out the right thing to do. If she went home, she wouldn't be in trouble, but there was no telling what Lauren would do. In the mood she was in, Kelly didn't doubt that she might go on the trip by herself. And she wasn't sure that Lauren would come back.

"All right," Kelly said at last. "I'll go. I still think it's the wrong thing, but I'll go."

"Thanks, Kel. We'll have fun, just wait and see."

"Yeah, well, I hope so. But I still don't see how we're going to keep from being shipped straight home as soon as we get there."

A smile came to Lauren's lips. "I can think of some pretty twisted ways to get there. If we don't have to check in with your dad until we get to Colorado, we might have longer than you think."

"Just as long as you don't try to drive to Colorado by way of California," Kelly said. "That might be kind of hard to explain."

"We could still go to Florida, like I wanted to do in the first place." Lauren's face brightened, and she seemed to shake off her anger. "Anyway, at least we'll have the trip. I love to drive."

"I'm glad you do, because I sure don't." Kelly looked out the window at the shopping strips and gas stations that clustered around each exit of the highway. "How long is this going to take—assuming no detours through L.A.?"

"St. Louis to Denver is about twenty hours each way, I guess," Lauren said. "And we better figure on another couple of hours to get to the resort. If we drive hard, we should make it there sometime tomorrow."

Kelly sighed. Twenty-something hours each way, plus whatever time they took to eat or sleep. It was a long way to go just to get yelled at. "Promise me one thing, okay?"

"What's that?"

"Promise me that no matter what else happens, I get to make at least one run down the slopes."

11

Lauren raised her right hand like someone being sworn in for court. "I solemnly swear that Kelly Tallon will not end this spring break without getting a chance to ski."

"Good," Kelly said. "Now no matter what happens, it'll be worth it."

# TWO

Kelly jerked awake from a dream of falling. A radio was playing loudly, and she fumbled to her right, trying to find the switch to shut off the alarm. Her hand hit smooth glass. She blinked and pushed her hair back from her eyes. Then she remembered that she was in Lauren's car on the way to Colorado.

"You okay?" Lauren asked.

"Yeah. I've just never been very good at sleeping in cars."

Kelly sat up and looked through her window. They were passing fields where the brilliant green of spring wheat was just starting to poke through the brown earth. The sky overhead was a very dark gray and looked even darker ahead.

"Where are we?" she asked.

Lauren pulled a map from the space between the seats and passed it to Kelly. "I think we're about thirty miles from Kansas City. There's an exit coming up. See if you can find it on the map."

Kelly read the green sign on the road and ran her finger down the line of the interstate on the map until she found the small town she was looking for. "I don't think we've gone as far as you think. It looks more like fifty or sixty miles."

The dark sky caught Kelly's attention. Among the knots of gray cloud, there were streaks of greenish yellow that looked like bruises in the air. "Radio say anything about a storm?" she asked.

"Uh-uh."

"Looks like a big one up there. I'm surprised they haven't been saying anything."

"Nope," Lauren said. "But I've been listening to music stations."

Seconds later scattered drops of rain began to smash against the Mustang's windshield. Kelly leaned her face against the side window and looked up at the sky. The blackened clouds were heaving up and down. "Wow," she said. "It really looks bad."

Over the next few minutes the rain grew harder and the wind stronger. The sky got so dark that it was hard to believe that the sun hadn't set. Lauren barely slowed, even when they began to pass other cars that had pulled over to wait out the storm.

"You sure you can see okay?" Kelly asked.

"I can see," Lauren said. "As long as it doesn't get any worse." She had barely finished speaking when there was a sudden bang from the hood of the car. "What was that?"

There was another bang, and a sharp crack as something struck the windshield. Kelly saw a white lump glance off the fender of the car, and another bounce along the dark shoulder of the road.

"It's hail!" she shouted. "Big hail."

"It's going to beat my car to death," Lauren cried. There was another bang of hail against the roof, and another against the hood.

Kelly squinted through the gray sheets of wind-driven rain and hail. "It looks like there's a bridge over the road up ahead. If we can get under that . . ."

"You got it!" Lauren leaned far forward as she steered along a road that neither of them could clearly see. The sound of impacting hail increased until Kelly felt like she was inside a popcorn machine. The racket was deafening.

Just ahead the shadow of the bridge became visible. The second they slipped under it, the

15

deafening sound cut off as though someone had thrown a switch.

Lauren steered the car to the side of the road. For a second the girls just sat there, catching their breath. Kelly was breathing so hard, she felt as if she had pushed the car those last hundred yards down the highway.

"Look at the hood," Lauren said.

Kelly looked, and saw dozens of small circular dents in the sheet metal of the car's hood. She opened her door and stepped out, and Lauren did the same. "It's not too bad," Kelly said.

"Not bad? It's got more dents than a waffle!"

"When the sun comes out, it'll probably pop out most of them."

Lightning struck somewhere close by, and thunder boomed under the bridge like a bomb blast. Lauren and Kelly jumped. Kelly saw Lauren's eyes round and white against her tan skin. Lauren stared back for a moment, and then she surprised Kelly by bursting into laughter.

"What is wrong with you?" Kelly asked.

Lauren waved her hand and fought to hold down her laughter. "It's just . . . it's just that you looked so funny! With your eyes popping out and everything."

Kelly shook her head. "You're nuts."

16

"I know," Lauren said. She managed to strangle the last bit of her laughter just as another clap of thunder shook the ground under their feet. Somewhere in the distance, a high-pitched siren began to blow. "What's that? Fire engine? Something started by the lightning?"

"I don't think so," Kelly said after a moment. "I think it's a tornado warning."

Lauren tilted her head back and looked upward. "Great. What is this, some kind of sign? Well, it's not going to work. I'm going on this trip, and that's that." Lightning flashed close by and they both jumped again.

"At least I don't see any tornado coming," Kelly said. They leaned against the car and watched as the hail pounded on the roadway beyond the bridge. Every now and then a gust of wind brought some of the rain almost to their feet, and the girls flinched every time the thunder crashed. A single car went zipping past them so quickly that they barely saw it before it had vanished behind the wall of rain and hail.

"There's somebody in a hurry," Kelly said.

"And somebody that doesn't care about their car," Lauren added.

A few minutes later the lightning began to lessen and the distant wail of the siren went

17

away. The hail vanished, and the rain settled down to a steady drizzle. Most of the storm seemed to have passed to the east, leaving a gray, overcast sky in the west that promised days of rain.

"Think we should go now?" Kelly asked.

"I guess so." Lauren opened the driver's door and started to get in.

"Lauren," Kelly said softly.

Lauren leaned back out. "What?"

"Maybe we should go home. I mean, this isn't exactly the best way to start a trip. And with your dad and everything. Maybe it *is* some kind of sign."

Lauren ran a hand through her short hair. Kelly could see that the resolve she had shown that morning had been eroded by the storm. But finally she shook her head. "No, let's go on."

"Do you really think we should?" Kelly asked.

"Of course I do. Just wait," Lauren replied. "Good things are going to start to happen soon."

The storm had filled the ditches at the side of the road with rivers of surging water and turned the green fields into dark-brown mud. Kelly saw some trees down beside a distant white house and a truck mired in the water-choked ruts of a dirt road.

They had gone only a few miles when they

passed a green sedan on the side of the road. It was an old car, and its squared-off sides showed the dents of the hailstorm. The hood was up, and as they went past, a figure waved at them from the driver's window.

Lauren slowed and turned her head to look back at the car. "Is that the car that passed us while we were waiting?"

Kelly thought for a moment. "I'm not sure. It could be."

Lauren pulled over to the side of the road, stopped, and shifted the Mustang into reverse. "Let's see what his trouble is."

"Why don't we just go on to the next exit and tell somebody to come back for him?" Kelly asked. "It might not be such a great idea to stop out here in the middle of nowhere."

"Come on, Kel. If we want good things to happen, we have to do good things, right?"

"Sounds right," Kelly agreed. "But let's do good things someplace else, okay?"

Lauren kept backing up. The green sedan appeared through the haze of the drizzle, and the driver got out and started jogging toward the Mustang. Lauren rolled down the window as he approached.

"Thanks for stopping," the guy said. "I was afraid I would be stuck here for hours."

From the passenger seat Kelly couldn't see

the man very well. A strong chin, slightly curly dark hair, a flash of white teeth between smiling lips—that was all. But she didn't have to see him to know what he looked like; Lauren's response told her everything.

Lauren tilted her head slightly and put on a knowing smile. "I'm just glad we could help," she said. Her voice was half an octave lower than normal and it oozed sophistication. "Do you want us to send someone back for you?" She paused for a moment, and her smile widened. "Or maybe you'd like a ride to the next gas station?"

"I wouldn't want to cause you any trouble. . . ."

"It's no problem," Lauren said. "Climb in."

"Thanks," the man said. "Let me go lock up the car and get a couple of things, and I'll be right back." He trotted back down the rainy highway.

"I still think this is a bad idea," Kelly said.

Lauren turned to her and raised an eyebrow. "Did you get a good look at him?"

"Not really."

"Just wait till you do."

"Look," Kelly said. "I'm sure he's cute, but shouldn't we just send someone for him? I mean, it's not safe to pick people up off the side of the road."

"Relax. It's only until the next exit."

20

Kelly started to make one last protest, but she was interrupted by a rapping against her window. She turned to see the guy looking in at her.

At first she thought Lauren was wrong—there was nothing special about him. He was average. He was young, maybe no older than they were, maybe college age. His faded letter jacket fit loosely over a trim build. *Okay*, she thought, *he is pretty good-looking, but nothing to get all that worked up about*. Then Kelly saw his eyes.

His eyes were blue. Not blue like most blue eyes, but an incredibly deep blue like sapphires. Those eyes transformed his face.

Without thinking about it, Kelly pushed her door open and climbed out into the drizzle. She felt nervous, as if the guy was going to ask her out instead of bumming a ride in Lauren's car. "Uh, the backseat's pretty cramped," she said. "Maybe I better ride back there."

"No," he said. "It's enough that you're giving me a ride. I'm not going to kick you out of your seat. I'll be fine in the back."

Kelly stood aside as he pulled her seat forward and slid into the small rear seat of the Mustang. "You're sure you fit okay?" she asked as she climbed back into the front.

"I'm fine," he said. Kelly got another flash of his very white teeth as he gave her a quick

21

smile. Then he turned toward Lauren. "I really appreciate you ladies rescuing me like this."

"We're happy to help," Lauren said. "You have everything you need out of your car?"

He held up a small leather satchel in his right hand. "Right here."

"Then let's get going." Lauren hit the gas and shifted the gears as the Mustang sped up. The rain had dropped off enough to crank the wipers down to intermittent. In the distance a dull orange glow at the base of the clouds showed that the sun had almost set.

"My name's Marshall," the man said as they left the green sedan behind. Kelly thought there was something unusual in his voice. Maybe it was a trace of a southern accent, maybe it was just his relaxed, slow way of talking. Whatever it was, it made her feel comfortable.

Lauren spoke up. "Hi, Marshall, I'm Lauren." She took one hand off the wheel and stretched her arm toward the backseat to exchange a quick shake.

Kelly turned in her seat. "Kelly." She reached out her hand, and Marshall took it. He held it for a long moment between fingers that were strong and had the slight roughness that came from hard work.

"You girls on vacation?" he asked.

"How'd you guess?" Lauren asked.

"Spring break?"

"Yeah," Lauren said. "You too?"

"You got it. Let me guess, you two are . . . juniors?"

"Seniors," Lauren told him.

"Wow, seniors. What college?"

"Oh, we're still in high school," Kelly said.

Lauren glanced over at her with a look that could have cut glass, and Kelly realized that she had just stomped on the image Lauren had been constructing. "But only for one more month," she finished weakly.

"I never would have guessed you were still in high school," Marshall said. "You look older."

Kelly could feel the blood rise in her face and hoped her blush wasn't obvious in the dim light. She knew he was talking only about Lauren. No one had ever thought Kelly looked older than she was. Younger all the time, but never older.

"What about you?" Lauren asked. "Are you in college?"

"I just finished up a premed program," Marshall said. "I guess I'll start med school in the fall, but I'm still trying to decide where."

Kelly was surprised. She wouldn't have thought Marshall was old enough to be out of college already, and his clothes, car, and rough

23

hands didn't match her idea of a medical student. But maybe he had gotten through school on a scholarship. And if he was as young as he looked, maybe he had been one of those genius kids that started college years early. Or maybe, like Kelly, he just looked younger than he was.

"Have you made college plans yet, Lauren?" Marshall asked.

"Well, if it were up to me, I'd be heading for the West Coast. But my dad wants me back east somewhere."

"Well, if you'll excuse me for giving advice, I don't think you should listen to your dad. The West Coast is a great place to be in college."

"My dad thinks that the Ivy League schools are the only place to get a good education," Lauren said.

"Maybe fifty years ago," Marshall said, "but not today. Go where you want to go. You're only in college once. Why spend four years in a place you don't want to be?"

"I wish my dad could hear you say that! He won't listen to me, but a med student that's been to those schools . . . Maybe he'd listen to you."

"Hey, if you think it would help, I'll be happy to give him a call."

Lauren began to talk about her father and all the things he'd put her through. For the most part Marshall listened quietly, interjecting a comment every now and then or asking a few questions. He gave the impression that he was hanging on her every word.

Kelly felt left out. She looked for a chance to get back in the conversation, but Lauren was on a roll, and Kelly couldn't get a word in edgewise. She leaned her head against the cool glass of the window and watched the darkening countryside roll past.

A few minutes later the car sped over a gentle rise. A mile up the road was an exit ramp, and just a few hundred yards from the intersection was a sprawling truck stop.

"Look," Kelly said. "There's a place we can see about getting a tow."

Lauren stopped her story about her father in midsentence and turned to look at the approaching truck stop. "I don't know. That place doesn't look like they'd notice anything that had less than a dozen wheels. They might not even have a tow truck."

"We'd better check," Kelly said. "We're probably twenty miles from Marshall's car already. If we go any farther, it'll cost him a fortune to tow it."

"Kelly's right," Marshall said. "We'd better stop."

Lauren pursed her lips, but she nodded and guided the car onto the exit ramp. There were a dozen semis clustered around the pumps and washing bays of the truck stop. Lauren steered through the giant metal tractor trailers toward the service station. At the entrance Lauren spotted a small restaurant.

"Why don't we get something to eat first?" she suggested. "We haven't stopped in hours."

Kelly didn't want to eat at this place. The white brick walls of the building had been splashed with mud from the passing trucks, and the inside didn't look much cleaner. But she realized that what Lauren wanted was not a chance to eat but an excuse to spend a few more minutes with Marshall. "Okay," she said. "Sounds good."

They climbed out of the car and Kelly stretched, trying to work the stiffness of the long ride out of her arms and legs. The door opened and one of the truckers inside the restaurant came out. He was a potbellied man with arms as big as hams and dark hair that was streaked with gray. He had his arm tight around the waist of a pretty girl that looked to be high-school age or younger.

"Are you sure you're going all the way to L.A.?" the girl asked.

"Sure, honey," said the tall man. "Don't you want to get to California?"

"I guess," the girl said. She followed the man to one of the parked trucks and he boosted her up into the cab. Kelly couldn't hear the rest of their conversation, but she could hear the man laughing as he climbed in. She thought the girl was pretty stupid—or pretty desperate—to get in that truck, and she wondered if the girl would ever see L.A.

"Let's get inside," Lauren said.

Kelly nodded and followed Marshall and Lauren into the small restaurant. There was a sign over the largest part of the room that said TRUCK DRIVERS ONLY. What was left was a pair of booths crammed into the space beside the kitchen door.

"I think we better sit over there," Marshall said. "No one is going to mistake you two for truck drivers."

Kelly thought about the girl in the parking lot. No one would have taken her for a truck driver either.

Marshall waited while the two girls slipped into a booth, then took a seat next to Lauren. "Cheer up," he said to Kelly. "The food in these places is usually pretty good."

Kelly took a plastic menu from the rack at the back of the table and looked over the options. It was the expected collection of sandwiches and dinner plates.

The waitress, a middle-aged woman in a faded blue uniform, came over to the table. "You ready to order?" she asked.

"Burger and fries," Lauren said without looking at the menu.

"Sounds good," Marshall said. "I'll have the same."

Kelly scanned the menu, trying to find something that wasn't drenched in grease. "Can I just get a green salad?"

"Sure," the waitress said. She scribbled their order on her pad. "Be up in just a minute."

As she walked away, Marshall stood. "While we're waiting for our food, I think I'll go check on getting my car towed. Okay?"

"Okay," Lauren said. "Want me to come with you?"

"You better wait," he said. "I'll be right back." He went to the front of the restaurant and shoved the glass door open. He waited a moment, holding the door while a man in a green T-shirt came in and walked into the truck drivers' section of the little restaurant. As he slipped out the door, Marshall turned to flash one last smile.

"What do you think?" Lauren said as soon as the door had closed.

"About what?" Kelly asked.

"You know. About Marshall."

Kelly picked up a saltshaker shaped like a tiny truck and turned it around in her hand. "I don't know. He's cute."

28

"He's more than cute," Lauren said. "Way more. And he's a med student."

"Yeah, he's really nice, but what does it matter? We're going to Colorado, and he's going . . . wherever it is he's going."

Lauren frowned for a moment. "You know, I don't think we ever talked about that. I wonder where he is going?"

"Good evenin'," said a voice.

Kelly looked up and saw the trucker in the green shirt standing above them. He was well over six feet tall, and his shoulders were thick with muscle. A baseball cap was pulled low over his dark-blond hair. His gray eyes were fixed on Lauren. "You need a ride tonight, little lady?" he asked.

Lauren looked up at him in confusion. "Ride?"

"We don't need a ride," Kelly said. "Thanks anyway."

The trucker's eyes shifted over to Kelly and scanned her as if he were seeing her for the first time. "I wasn't asking you, kid." He turned back to Lauren. "Come on, sugar. Let's go for a ride in a big rig." He reached down a large hand to Lauren.

She leaned away from him. "I've . . . I've got a car," she sputtered.

"A car's only a car," he said. His beefy fingers

29

closed on her shoulder and he let his hand drift across the soft material of her sweater.

Kelly reached across the table and grabbed his arm. "We're just waiting for a friend."

The trucker didn't bother to look at her this time. "Don't worry. I can be friendly."

Lauren looked over at Kelly. Her dark eyes, usually so confident, seemed lost.

Kelly looked around for the waitress, for some other customers, for anybody. But the room was empty. She started to push herself up from her seat. She wasn't sure what she could do against this guy, but she had to do something.

Kelly had just stood up, when the glass door of the restaurant swung open and Marshall came striding in. His deep-blue eyes locked on the trucker. "What's the problem here?" he asked.

The trucker looked up. "There's no problem here, sonny. I was just taking this lady for a ride."

Marshall took two slow steps toward the table. "Maybe the lady doesn't want a ride."

"Butt out," the trucker said, but he took his hand off of Lauren and straightened up to face Marshall. "This is none of your business, boy."

Marshall took another step. He was no more than three feet from the trucker. Kelly could see the muscles in the trucker's arms knotting as he clinched his hands into fists.

30

"Lauren," Marshall said softly. "Did this man hurt you?"

"No," Lauren said.

"Not yet," Kelly added.

"Then everything's okay." Marshall nodded his head toward the empty trucker's side of the restaurant. "If you could just go back to your seat, we can go on with our dinner."

"Sure," the trucker said. "As soon as the lady tells me herself. I'm going to—" started the trucker.

Marshall's hand pistoned out as fast as a striking snake and hit the bigger man in the chest. The trucker's gray eyes bugged out and he staggered backward. A honking noise came from his mouth as he fought to pull in a breath.

Marshall turned to Kelly. "Why don't you take Lauren out to the car," he said. His voice was still so very calm, completely unhurried, but there was something in his eyes—a light that hadn't been there before. "I'll find the waitress and see if I can get our food to go."

The trucker managed to pull in a long whistling breath. He coughed. "You son of a—"

Marshall hit him again. This time the big man didn't just stagger—he fell like a puppet with its strings cut.

"Is he okay?" Kelly asked.

"He'll be fine in a few minutes," Marshall said. "I just hit him in the solar maxus. Come on, there's no tow truck here. Let's just forget the waitress and get something at another place." He held out a hand to Lauren, and she took it quickly.

She climbed to her feet and followed him toward the door. They were almost out before she turned back to Kelly. "You coming, Kel?" she asked.

"Sure. I'll be right there." Kelly watched them go out the door, then took a look at the man on the floor. She was relieved when he finally groaned and turned over on his side.

At the front door, she paused and watched Marshall guiding Lauren across the wet parking lot. Kelly might have had only high-school biology, but she knew that the place where Marshall had punched the guy was called the solar plexus, not the solar maxus.

*Would a guy that had graduated premed make a mistake like that?* Kelly didn't know. She pushed open the door and walked out.

# THREE

"Sorry to keep you running around like this," Marshall said.

"Are you kidding?" Lauren said. "After the way you took care of that jerk at the truck stop, you deserve a medal or something."

"It's really unfortunate that this had to happen. You know, most truckers are really decent guys. Don't let this give you a bad impression of them."

"You think this next place will have a towing service?" Kelly asked.

"That's what they said at the last place," Marshall replied.

Since leaving the truck stop, they had been to three other places along the interstate. One even had a tow truck parked in front, but Marshall had come back out saying that the truck was broken. By now they were getting close to Kansas City, and Marshall's old green sedan was thirty or forty miles back down the road. Kelly was beginning to wonder if they would ever find a place to go back for it.

"Where are you going, anyway, Marshall?" Kelly asked.

"Just on my way to visit some friends out west," he replied.

Kelly waited for him to go on, but that seemed to be all he was going to say. "Sounds nice. Where at?"

"Oh, some different places," he said. "Hey, there's our exit."

At this exit the road was lined with fast-food places and a couple of cheap motels. There were two gas stations, but neither of them had a garage or any sign of a towing service.

"You sure this is the place?" Kelly asked.

"Just following directions," Marshall said.

"They probably told you the wrong thing back at that last place," Lauren added. "Should we go on to the next exit?"

Kelly groaned to herself. She didn't care how cute this guy was or how much Lauren liked him. There was something strange about him, and she wanted him out of the car.

34

"Wait," Marshall said. "I just thought of something. Pull in at that gas station."

"Which one?"

"That one, the one with the minimart."

Lauren slid into the parking lot and pulled up next to the gas pumps. "As long as we're here, we might as well fill up. What did you think of?" she asked.

"The auto club," Marshall said. "I've got their card right here in my pocket. All I have to do is give them a call and they'll send someone to get my car. I don't know why I didn't think of it before."

"That's great!" Lauren said. "Will you need a ride someplace else?"

"I'll let you know as soon as I call," Marshall said. "And don't worry about the gas. I'll take care of it."

Kelly climbed out of the car so Marshall could get free of the backseat. She watched as he walked across the parking lot to a bank of pay phones on one side of the building. He pulled a wallet from the pocket of his jeans, glanced at something inside, and started dialing.

"Maybe we can finally get on with our trip," she said.

Lauren looked up from sticking the nozzle of the gas pump into the Mustang. "Why are

35

you in such a hurry? I like Marshall. Don't you?"

"Sure. He's fine."

Lauren squinted her dark eyes. "What's wrong, Kel? You've been acting like Marshall has three heads ever since we picked him up."

"I don't know," Kelly said. She shrugged her shoulders and tried to shake off her dark mood. She wanted to get back the excitement she had felt when the day started. "Let's just get on with our trip. You can get his phone number and get back to him later, but right now it's skiing time."

Lauren laughed. "I should have known," she said. "You and your skiing. Don't worry. I promised to get you on skis, didn't I?" She topped off the gas and hung up the hose. "You want anything to eat?"

"No, thanks. They never have anything but junk at these places. I'll wait."

"Well, I'm going to go grab a soda. Back in a sec."

Kelly checked on Lauren's makeshift ski rack. So far it seemed to be holding up fine. She leaned against the front of the car. It was chilly and the air was still damp from the storm. Despite the cool weather, a flurry of moths skittered around the fluorescent lighting at the edges of the lot. Standing there by herself, Kelly came closer to relaxing than she had in hours.

She heard footsteps and turned to see Marshall walking toward her from the phones. "Everything's taken care of," he said.

"They're going back for your car?" Kelly asked.

"They promised to get to it in about an hour, and they'll take it to a garage where it can be fixed."

"Sounds good, but don't you have to go with them? I mean, how will they get into your car?"

Marshall smiled. "It's an auto club. I'm sure they know what they're doing."

"I guess so," Kelly said. Whatever was going on, she was glad it was over.

Lauren came walking up with a can of soda. "Are they coming to get your car?" she asked Marshall.

"You bet," he said. "Everything's settled." He reached out and took Lauren's hand in his. "I really want to thank you for helping me out like this. I don't know what I would have done without you."

"Is there anything else we can do? Anywhere else you need to go?"

Marshall released her hand and sighed. "No, I guess not. It's just too bad I'm going to miss seeing my friends."

"Why's that?"

"Well, I was going to meet them in a couple of days, out in Denver. But by the time my car is fixed, they'll be gone."

Lauren's face brightened. "We're going through Denver! We could take you to meet your friends."

"I couldn't ask you to do that," Marshall said.

"Besides," Kelly added, "he wouldn't have any way to get back."

"Oh, getting back isn't a problem," Marshall said, "but I couldn't put you out like that."

"Sure you could," Lauren said with enthusiasm. "We don't mind at all."

"No, really. This is your vacation," Marshall said.

"Don't be silly! We don't mind, do we, Kelly?"

*Yes*, thought Kelly, *I mind a lot*. But what she said was: "No, you can ride with us."

Marshall gave a smile that seemed to reflect most of the light in the area. "Great! Really, you don't know how important this is to me."

Kelly closed her eyes and tried to convince herself it would be okay. After all, it was only one more day riding in a car. What could go wrong?

"If you're going to ride with us that far," she said, "you better get in front." This time Marshall didn't argue.

Kelly climbed into the back and folded herself into the small seat. Even as short as she was, it was cramped. When Marshall pushed the passenger seat back into place, Kelly felt like there was a wall between her and the others. The radio that had been just right in the front seat was so loud in the back that Kelly could barely hear Lauren and Marshall talking.

They were about a mile down the road before Kelly remembered something. "Lauren, did you pay for the gas?"

"What?"

"The gas!" Lauren leaned forward into the gap between the front seats. "Did you pay for the gas?"

"No," Lauren said. "Marshall took care of it."

Marshall nodded.

"No he didn't."

"What?"

"No he didn't!" Kelly almost shouted. "Marshall didn't even go inside the store." Marshall said something that Kelly didn't understand. "What?" she called. "Lauren, can you turn down the radio? I can't hear what you're saying."

Lauren turned down the radio. "Marshall says it's okay," she said.

Kelly looked back and forth between them.

"Okay? Lauren, he didn't pay for the gas. We have to go back and pay for it."

"Don't worry about it," Marshall said. "People forget all the time. Places like that expect to lose a few. They just add it to their prices."

Kelly tried to ignore him and talk to Lauren. "It's stealing, Lauren. We've got to go back and pay."

Lauren started to answer, but Marshall spoke first. "Stealing? Do you know how much profit oil companies make off of stations like that? Do you really think their prices are fair?"

"What does that have to do with it?"

"These people make billions. They don't care about a tank of gas. They have the prices so jacked up that half the people in the place could leave without paying and they'd still make money." Marshall gave a little chuckle. "Don't cry for the oil companies. If anybody is stealing anything, it's them stealing money from all their customers."

Kelly tried to stay calm. "I'm not crying for any oil company, or even for the gas station. I just want to do what's right."

"Look," Marshall said. His calm voice was really starting to get on Kelly's nerves. "It's probably ten miles to the next exit. And by then, you're going to be in the city, and it'll probably take you an hour just to get turned around." He glanced at the watch on his wrist. "It's getting close to ten now. By the time you get back here, it'll be midnight."

Kelly had to admit that spending two hours backtracking didn't sound like a lot of fun. When she and Lauren had planned the trip, they had thought they'd make it almost to Denver on the first day. But the storm and all the running around with Marshall had put them hours behind schedule.

"I don't want to waste time, but we should go back and pay for the gas," she said.

Marshall leaned over to Lauren and said something. Lauren nodded.

"What?" Kelly said. "What's he saying?"

"Marshall's right," Lauren said. "It's too big of a waste of time to go back."

"Lauren!"

"Come on, Kel. I thought you wanted to get to the slopes, right? I don't see any snow around here." She turned the radio back up, and Kelly was again cut off from the conversation.

Kelly fell back in her seat and gritted her teeth. *This was supposed to be our spring break,* she thought. *If Lauren just wanted to pick up guys, she could have done that without leaving home or dragging me along. This is turning out to be one great vacation.*

41

Traffic increased as they rolled into the city. Lauren guided the Mustang between rows of trucks and cars, using the car's big engine to blast past knots of slow-moving traffic. Lauren and Marshall kept up a conversation all the time. Kelly could see Marshall waving his hands as he explained some point, and several times she heard Lauren laughing at something he had said.

Kelly leaned her face against the side of the car and watched the lights sweep past. From the elevated interstate, the neighborhoods were laid out in neat rows. Lines of street lamps gleamed green or amber or white. When they passed the downtown area, the tall buildings were topped with flashing lights. Kelly spotted several night-clubs where people milled by the door and strobe lights beat against the windows.

She stopped trying to hear what Lauren and Marshall were talking about and just watched things go by. She liked traveling at night. In the day everything looked so normal, so ordinary. But at night it was easy for Kelly to imagine that she was crossing some foreign country and the lights out there might have been London or Paris, not Kansas City.

# FOUR

The lights grew sparser as they moved west. Instead of the sparkling clusters of the city, Kelly saw only the isolated lights of an occasional farm. The farmhouses all looked ghostly white, and the clumps of trees that surrounded each house seemed old and evil. The clouds were beginning to break up, and a yellow moon hung low in the west, casting dim shadows across the flat land.

Kelly didn't realize she was dozing off until Marshall shook her awake. "We need to stop somewhere," he said. He had to say it again before Kelly's head cleared enough to understand him. Her half-formed dreams evaporated, and she became aware of the cramped confines of the backseat.

43

"Stop?" she said.

"It's getting pretty late," Marshall explained. "We need to find a place to sleep for the night."

Kelly was disapointed to be stopping this far from their goal, but she didn't want Lauren driving if she was getting tired. "Sure. Whenever Lauren wants to pull over."

For long miles, the dark fields rolled by and the highway went on without any sign of an exit. And when an exit did come up, there was no motel. By the time they reached an exit that did have a motel, Kelly was half dozing again.

The motel was new, one of those buildings built from modules that could be assembled in a matter of days. Its square white sides looked alien against the dark Kansas fields. A red sign at the front flashed VACANCY.

"We could get one room," Marshall said. "It's cheaper that way."

"Sounds okay to me," Lauren said.

Kelly tried to shake the cobwebs out of her head. "I'd rather not."

Lauren stopped the car by the office door and cut the engine. "Come on, Kel. We'd have two beds."

"Sorry. I just wouldn't be comfortable."

Lauren's forehead creased in irritation. "First

44

the gas and now this. You're starting to sound like my mother."

Marshall held up his hands. "It's okay," he said. "We'll get two rooms. I don't want to cause any trouble."

Lauren shot Kelly another dark look, but she didn't argue. It took only a few minutes to get their rooms from a sleepy clerk. Kelly dragged her heavy suitcase from Lauren's car and wrestled it across the parking lot. Lauren handled her case with more ease.

Marshall waited there for them at the door to their room. He jerked his thumb at a restaurant on the other side of the parking lot. "That chain usually has a pretty good breakfast. You want to meet there in the morning?"

Lauren smiled at him. "Sounds good. About eight?"

"See you then," he said. He took two steps away, then turned back. "I'll be in room one fourteen if you need me."

"Do you have everything you need?" Lauren asked. "I think I've got some spare shampoo and stuff like that."

Marshall held up his small brown bag. "Nope. I've got everything I need right here."

"Good night!" Lauren called.

She opened the door and held it while Kelly pulled her bag inside. As soon as the door was shut, Lauren turned on Kelly. "What is your problem?"

"Come on, Lauren," Kelly said. "Let's not do this now. I'm tired."

The motel room looked like any of a million others: twin beds, a small table, some cabinets, and a television on a metal stand. The paintings on the wall were abstract jumbles of red and blue.

"I'm tired too," Lauren said. "I'm the one that's been driving all day." She tossed her suitcase onto one of the beds. "What have you got against Marshall?"

"I don't have anything against Marshall," Kelly replied. She sat on the edge of the bed. More than anything, she just wanted to go to sleep and get this day over with.

"Then why are you always arguing with him?"

"I'm not arguing with him. It's just that I don't think it's a good idea to steal things."

"We didn't steal anything! It was just an accident."

"Whatever," Kelly said. "Please, can we just go to bed?"

"What about the room?" Lauren insisted. "Why didn't you let him share a room with us?"

"We just met the guy this afternoon. Why

46

should we share a motel room with him?"

"There you go again! You treat him like he's a mass murderer or something. Marshall's a great guy."

Kelly opened her suitcase and searched through the folded clothes for her nightshirt. "What makes him so great? You don't know anything about him."

"Are you kidding? We've been talking for hours. I probably know him better than any of the guys in our class. He's . . . he's . . ." Lauren waved her hands, searching for the right words. "He's so different from all those high-school guys." She opened her suitcase, took out a smaller bag, and headed for the bathroom.

"He's different all right," Kelly said.

Lauren stopped and looked back at her. "And what is that supposed to mean?"

"Nothing."

"All I meant was, he listens to me. When I talk, I feel like he's really paying attention. High-school guys never listen." Lauren walked into the bathroom.

"Your dad never listens either," Kelly said, but she said it too softly for Lauren to hear. She raised her voice. "I just don't know what difference this makes. Even if he does ride with us to Denver, we're only going to see him for another day. Then he'll be gone."

"Right," Lauren called. "Can't you be nice to him for one day?"

"I have been nice to him."

"Oh, yeah. Don't think he hasn't noticed how you're treating him." Kelly heard Lauren unzip her small case. A moment later the sound of running water came from the bathroom.

Kelly bit back a sharp remark. Irritation was starting to outweigh her sleepiness. "Did he say something about me?"

"He just wants you to like him, Kel. He can't figure out why you don't. I mean, look what he did for us at the truck stop."

"What he did for us? What he did was beat up a guy and almost kill him. I don't know why that makes you think Marshall's some kind of hero."

Lauren stuck her head out of the bathroom. "Now I know you're crazy. That guy he hit could have done anything. Didn't you see how he was looking at me?"

"That guy didn't do anything but put a hand on your shoulder," Kelly said. "Marshall hit him first."

"He was only trying to protect me." Lauren stepped out of the bathroom with her toothbrush in one hand. "Would you be happier if he'd let that guy take me away? Or let himself get killed?"

"You know I don't want that."

"No, Kel. I don't know what you want."

Kelly closed her eyes and fell back on the bed. "I want things to be okay. I want us to get on with our trip. I want to go skiing."

"That's your problem," Lauren said. "All you ever think of is yourself."

"Oh, absolutely," Kelly said. "That's why I haven't called home like I was supposed to tonight." She opened one eye and looked over toward Lauren. "Please, we only have to get along with Marshall for one day, but you and I have been friends for years. Can't we get along?"

Lauren was silent for a moment. "We can talk about it again in the morning." She stomped back into the bathroom, making no effort to hide her anger.

Kelly sighed and forced herself to get up from the bed. She kicked off her shoes and sat down to peel off her socks. Once she had pulled off her clothes and slipped into her nightshirt, she felt better. She pulled the covers from the bed and slid into the cool sheets.

The shower kicked on in the bathroom. Kelly lay for a few minutes, replaying the events of the day. After a while she decided that maybe she was overreacting. As soon as Lauren came out of the shower, Kelly would apologize. After all, what could it hurt? But long before the shower stopped, Kelly was asleep.

49

*        *        *

Kelly woke and sat up in bed. Her breath was coming fast, and sweat glinted on her forehead. As soon as she had fallen asleep, the nightmares had started. They were a jumble of Lauren's face, the blue Mustang, and Marshall. But they made no sense. They were only dark, confusing images from which Kelly understood nothing but overwhelming fear.

There was a moment of confusion before she remembered where she was. The room was dark. The only light was what little filtered through the blinds from the parking lot outside. She looked over at Lauren's bed, saw the dark form lying there, and relaxed a little.

"Everything's okay," she whispered to herself. "Go back to sleep." She started to lie down. Then she took a better look at Lauren's bed.

Lauren wasn't in it.

The dark form she had seen was only Lauren's suitcase, her pillow, and the rumpled blankets. Not trusting her own eyes, Kelly got up and leaned over the vacant bed where Lauren should have been. She ran a hand over the empty sheets.

"Lauren?" Kelly said quietly. She crept around the corner toward the bathroom. The door was open and the inside of the room was

50

dark. "Lauren?" she said more loudly. There was no reply.

Kelly walked quickly to the front of the room and flipped on the lights. Lauren was definitely not in the room, and it didn't take much thought to figure out where she was. The only question was what Kelly should do about it.

She opened the front door a crack and peeked outside. A cold draft came through the opening. The parking lot was only about half full, and fresh puddles showed that it had rained while Kelly slept. It was very quiet. The restaurant across the parking lot was dark, and even the highway seemed empty.

Kelly looked down the side of the motel toward room one fourteen. Marshall's room was only a few doors away. It would be easy to go there and knock on the door.

"Yeah," she whispered to herself. "And no matter what's going on in there, I'll end up looking like an even bigger jerk than I already do."

Kelly stepped back and shut the door on the cold Kansas night. Going to Marshall's room was definitely a bad idea. If Lauren was there, she'd be furious with her. If she wasn't there, then Kelly would have to explain herself to Marshall.

51

She dropped onto her bed. She wasn't sure what had made Lauren so attracted to Marshall. Lauren never had trouble getting dates, and she wasn't the type to jump at the first guy that came along. But it had been a very long, very strange day. And with the problems Lauren had been having with her dad, it wasn't surprising that she wasn't acting normal.

*She's not an idiot. Lauren knows what she's doing and she can take care of herself.* Kelly wondered how many times she'd have to think that before she believed it.

She got back in bed and pulled the sheets up. The motel room suddenly felt very cold and empty. She could hear a truck going past out on the highway. Somehow the sound only made the silence of the room seem thicker.

Lauren was right about one thing: Kelly did not trust Marshall. He was just too smooth, too quick with an answer to everything. Over and over Kelly kept coming back to the fight with the trucker and the mistake Marshall had made in describing where he hit the man. Solar maxus. Solar plexus. It was a very small difference. And Marshall had been under stress. Everyone makes mistakes. But would a student going into medical school make a mistake like that?

The other thing that stuck in Kelly's mind was the strange light in Marshall's eyes when he actually hit the trucker.

"This is one great spring break." Kelly punched a fist into her pillow, turned over, and tried to sleep.

# FIVE

The nightmares didn't end when Kelly went back to bed. Her sleep came in troubled snatches that were darkened by wild images. Then, sometime after the window had begun to show the pearly light of approaching dawn, she turned over to see that Lauren was back in her bed. After that, sleep came easier.

"Kelly! Get up."

Kelly blinked her eyes against the light. Lauren was standing over her. She was already dressed in jeans and a violet turtleneck, and she looked agitated.

"What's wrong?" Kelly asked.

"We forgot to ask for a wake-up call," Lauren said. "It's already after eight. We need to meet Marshall and get on the road."

"Okay, but I need to take a shower."

Lauren frowned. "Why couldn't you have done that last night?"

"I was tired last night," Kelly said. "Look, I'm not hungry for breakfast. Why don't you go eat with Marshall, and you can come get me when you're done."

Kelly had expected Lauren to be happy to get a chance to be alone with Marshall, but instead she looked nervous. "Oh, okay," Lauren said. "I guess we can do that."

"What's wrong?"

"Nothing. It's just that . . ." Lauren stopped and shook herself. "I'm sure it'll be okay. I'll be back in a few minutes." She grabbed her purse from the table and hurried out the door.

Kelly wondered what had gone wrong the night before. She didn't think it could be too bad. Surely Lauren would have said something. But she was sure that the evening hadn't gone as Lauren had planned.

Kelly went to the window and peered around the edge of the blinds. The sky showed only a few clouds, but the trees were swaying from a strong breeze. People going into the restaurant were wearing sweaters or jackets. Kelly went back to her suitcase and searched for some warm clothing. She hadn't thought about it being that cold before they got to Colorado, so most of her heavy clothing was designed for the slopes, but she managed to find a light sweater to go with her jeans.

Kelly padded back across the carpet to the counter outside the bathroom and laid down her clothes. She slipped into the bathroom, stripped off her nightshirt, and stepped into the shower. The warm water sluiced over her and the soap smelled fresh and clean. By the time she'd washed her hair and rinsed herself, Kelly felt much better. With a good shower behind her, she was ready to get along with anybody.

She shut off the water and stepped out. As she did, she heard the door to the hotel room open, and a gust of cold air blew into the bathroom. She hugged her towel to her to ward off the chill.

"I'm just finishing my shower," she called. "I'll be out in a sec, Lauren." She toweled herself dry quickly and stepped over to the counter. With her hand reaching toward her clothes, she froze.

Marshall stood at the corner of the room, watching her. He had a wide smile on his face—the same gentle expression he had worn when they agreed to give him a lift. But his eyes were filled with the strange savage light Kelly had seen when he fought with the trucker.

It took Kelly a few moments to find her

voice. "Get out of here," she managed in a half-strangled whisper.

Marshall didn't get out, and he didn't reply. Instead he took a step closer. The smile stayed frozen on his face.

Kelly took a half step backward. She reached behind her with one hand, trying to find the bathroom door. With her other hand she held the towel tight against her. She was afraid to look down and see what it didn't cover.

"Get out," she said again. This time, despite all the fear tightening her stomach, Kelly was relieved to hear how firm her voice sounded. But Marshall didn't move.

Her fingers found the edge of the door. Kelly took two more steps backward and slammed the door. She went to lock it, then discovered that it didn't lock. She let the towel drop and pressed against the door with both hands. With the metal panel between them, much of her fear of Marshall was turned into anger. "Get out of my room!" she shouted.

There was the sound of movement. At first Kelly thought Marshall had decided to listen to her—that he was going away. Then his voice, his maddeningly calm voice, came from right outside the door. "I thought you were just a child, Kelly, but I was wrong. You're as much a woman as Lauren is."

Kelly shivered. "Please go away." There was only silence on the other side of the door.

It was several minutes before Kelly dared open the door again. When she did, there was no sign of Marshall. She tiptoed to the corner and looked around. The motel room was empty. Kelly ran across the room and locked every lock. Then she ran back to the bathroom and quickly pulled on her clothes.

She glanced at herself in the mirror. The sprinkling of freckles on her nose stood out against skin that had gone very pale. Her auburn hair was wet and tangled. She closed her eyes and took several deep breaths. She walked back to her suitcase and took out her comb and blow dryer.

The next time Kelly looked in the mirror, she liked what she saw a lot better. Her hair was dry and combed, her skin looked healthier, and her eyes had lost that scared-rabbit look. She nodded to herself and started to gather up her clothes to leave.

Then the door rattled. At once Kelly's heart leaped into overdrive. She walked toward the locked door. "Go away!" she shouted.

"Come on, Kel. We need to get going."

"Lauren!" Kelly quickly fumbled the locks open. Lauren was waiting outside the door with an amused smile on her face. Kelly stuck her

59

head out and looked around. "Where's Marshall?" she asked.

"He's already waiting in the car," said Lauren. "Are you ready to go?"

"Lauren, Marshall, he . . . he . . ."

"He walked in on you while you were getting dressed. Yeah, I know."

Kelly looked at her in amazement. "He told you?"

Lauren nodded. "He's really sorry, Kel. He thought you were ready."

"He's sorry? If he was sorry, then why didn't he leave when I told him to?"

A shadow of concern passed over Lauren's face and her smile faded. "I don't know. I guess he was as shocked as you were."

"Lauren, he wasn't shocked; he was staring."

"I'm sure he'll apologize. Come on, let's get going." She turned toward the car and started walking away.

Kelly jammed her hands into the pockets of her jeans. "No," she said.

Lauren stopped and looked back over her shoulder. "What do you mean, no?"

"I mean no," Kelly said. "I'm not riding in a car with that guy."

"What are you going to do, stay here?"

"If I have to. I'll take a bus home or call my dad, but I'm not going anywhere with Marshall."

Lauren took two steps back toward Kelly. "Yeah, well, you'll be happy to hear that Marshall's only going with us for a couple of miles. He's made some kind of plans to get where he's going another way."

"Really? Did he tell you that last night?"

"No, he told me this . . ." Lauren's dark eyes narrowed. "How could he have told me anything last night?"

"I meant in the car," Kelly said quickly. It wouldn't do any good to confront Lauren about being absent from her bed—especially if Marshall had already dumped her. "It's hard to hear in the backseat," she added.

"Oh," Lauren said. "Well, are you going with us? Or are you going to stay here in middle of Nowhere, U.S.A.?"

"As long as it's only for a few miles."

Lauren turned without another word and stomped off toward the car. Kelly went back inside and grabbed her suitcase. She took a look around the room to make sure they hadn't forgotten anything, then shut the door for the last time.

Both Marshall and Lauren were waiting beside the car when Kelly walked up. Marshall stepped forward to help with her suitcase. Kelly held on to it for a second, but she let Marshall take it and heave it into the trunk of the Mustang.

"I'm sorry about walking in on you," he said.

Kelly stared into Marshall's sapphire eyes. He seemed so embarrassed and sincere, but she knew how he had acted in the room. "You're not riding all the way to Denver with us?" she asked.

Marshall shook his head sadly. "I'm sorry about that, too. But plans change."

Lauren wrapped her arms around herself and shivered. "You mind if we get going? It's freezing out here."

Kelly squeezed into the backseat and Marshall took his place in the front. Lauren cranked up the car and turned on the heat. They rolled around to the front of the motel, and Lauren got out to turn in the keys. Kelly waited for Marshall to say something while Lauren was out of the car, but he stayed facing the front of the car and didn't say a word until she came back.

"I just need to go back to the last exit," Marshall said. "My friend is going to pick me up there."

"Why not this exit?" Kelly asked.

"I'm afraid I gave him the wrong place when we were on the phone. But it's only a couple of miles back; it won't take long."

"Let's get it over with," Lauren said.

*Amen*, Kelly thought.

The wind was getting very gusty. Kelly could

62

feel it pushing against the car as they got out on the interstate and headed east. They passed a line of cars that had streamers of crepe paper dangling from their bumpers and hand-lettered signs in the windows. SPRING BREAK said one sign. FLORIDA! read another.

"Maybe they've got the right idea," Kelly said as they passed the last of the Florida-bound cars. "Maybe we should have gone to the beach like everybody else."

"You can't blame me for that one, Kel. This spring-skiing business was your idea."

It was farther back to the exit than Marshall had said, and it took them about twenty minutes to get there. When they arrived, there was only a single gas station and a dusty sign pointing up a pothole-scarred state road.

"You sure this is the place?" Lauren asked.

"Yes," Marshall said. "Just drop me off over there at the station."

Lauren pulled in beside the pumps. "We're almost out of gas again. We better fill up, or we'll have to stop in ten minutes."

Everyone piled out of the car, and there was an awkward moment as they all stood around in the parking lot. It was Marshall who spoke up first. "I really can't thank you girls enough for helping me out. You've done so much more than you had to."

"Yeah, well. Take care of yourself," Lauren said.

"Here," Marshall said, "take this." He held out a slip of greenish paper that was topped by the logo of the motel where they'd spent the night.

"What's this?"

"I wrote my address and phone number on it. When you get back from vacation, give me a call. We'll get together."

Lauren's gloomy expression brightened a little. "Okay, I will."

Marshall extended his hand to Kelly. "And thanks for your help too."

Kelly took his hand and gave it a fast shake. "I hope your ride shows up soon."

"Don't worry," Marshall said. "I'll be out of here in no time." He turned toward the door of the gas station, then turned back. "And don't worry about the gas. I'll pay." Kelly already had her purse out and she started to protest, but Marshall held up a hand. "Really," he said. "I'll take care of it. You guys just get going and have a great spring break."

"Bye," Lauren called.

Marshall gave a final wave and disappeared into the station. Lauren flipped the lid from her gas tank, and Kelly helped her get the hose in place.

"You ready to get on with the trip?" Kelly asked as the pump registered the gallons flowing into the tank.

"Yeah," Lauren said softly. Then she looked up and smiled. "Yeah, I am. And I'm sorry if I was a jerk last night."

"You weren't a jerk," Kelly said. "I was. I shouldn't have made such a big deal about Marshall."

"No, you were right. There was no point getting so worked up about a guy I'll probably never see again."

"You've got his address. Maybe you will see each other again."

"Maybe," Lauren said. "Friends again?"

"We never stopped being friends," Kelly said. The gas pump snapped off and Kelly looked toward the station. "Think we should go inside and pay for it?"

"Marshall said he'd take care of it. Let's believe him this time."

They piled into the car and rolled out to the edge of the parking lot. Kelly stretched out her legs, relishing the space of the front seat. "Skiing, here we come! Uh-oh."

"What?" Lauren said.

"I left my purse back there on the gas pump."

"You're lucky we're out here in the boonies, or someone would have it by now." Lauren

65

shifted the car into reverse and eased back to the side of the pumps.

"There it is," Kelly said. "It's right where I left it." She opened her door to get her purse.

Lauren stepped out too. "I think I'll go get a soda before we go," Lauren said.

"I don't know how you can drink those things in the morning," Kelly said. "Cola before noon, bleh!"

"What is life without caffeine?" Lauren asked with a laugh. "I'll just run in and get a couple of cans. You want anything?"

"Nope. Like I said, all they have at these places is soda and junk food. I'll wait until lunch."

"Back in a second!"

Kelly hopped back in the car and pulled the highway map out of the glove box. She found their location on the map and frowned at the long gap between where they were and where they wanted to be. Maybe she could convince Lauren to let her do some driving. If they took turns and stayed on the road all night, they could still be at the slopes before dawn.

There was a loud thump from the front of the car. Startled, Kelly dropped the map and saw Lauren leaning against the hood of the car. She was facing the station, holding herself up with a hand on the hail-dented hood of the Mustang.

Her normally tan skin was gray as stone. Beyond her, the door to the station swung slowly closed on its hinges.

Kelly pushed open her door. "Lauren? Lauren, are you okay?"

Lauren turned toward Kelly. Her dark eyes were dull and unfocused. Her hand slipped over the blue hood of the car, and she began to fall. Kelly struggled to release her seat belt and get out, but before she could, Lauren had toppled to the ground.

Kelly ran around the car and knelt beside Lauren. "Lauren! What happened?"

There was a crash from the station as the front door flew open. Marshall stepped out into the sunlight. His face was as calm as ever, but his blue eyes were blazing. His brown satchel dangled from his left hand. "What are you two doing back here?" he said in a cold voice.

Anger swept through Kelly. She looked up at him. "What did you do to Lauren?"

Marshall took a long step closer. "Why did you come back?" he said.

Kelly started to stand. "Answer my question, you son of—"

Marshall moved much faster than Kelly had expected; faster than she would have believed. He crossed the parking lot in a flash, and his long fingers bit into Kelly's shoulder as he pulled her to her feet. She felt the blood drain from her face. He pulled again, and Kelly felt her tennis shoes leave the ground as he held her out like a rag doll.

"Be very careful what you say," Marshall said. He spoke quietly, and there was no emotion in his voice, but it was more frightening than any mad screaming that Kelly had ever heard. He dropped her and she fell to her knees.

Marshall looked down at them. "To answer your question, I did nothing to her." He took a few steps away and stared off at the highway.

Kelly's heart was beating so hard that it made her head ring. She lifted Lauren's head and saw that her eyes were open. Tears streamed down her cheeks. "Get up!" Kelly whispered urgently. "We've got to get out of here."

Lauren put her hand on the bumper of the Mustang, and Kelly helped her up. She had almost made it to the door of the car when Marshall turned back to them. "Put her in the back," he said. "I want you to drive." When Kelly didn't move, he grabbed her by the arm and shoved her against the car. "Do it now."

Kelly scrambled away. "No! I'm not doing anything for you." She backed away, looking around for anything to use as a weapon.

"Obviously," Marshall said, "I'm not making myself clear." He reached into his satchel and pulled out a pistol. But he didn't point it at Kelly. He went over to where Lauren still leaned against the car and spun her around to face Kelly. Then he put the muzzle of the gun into the short black hair at the back of Lauren's head.

"Get in and drive or I'll blow your sexy friend's brains out." He wrapped his other arm around Lauren's throat and pulled her tight against his chest. "There. Is that clear enough?"

Tears were still sliding down Lauren's face, and her body jerked as she sobbed silently. Kelly licked her dry lips. "All right," she said. "I'll drive. Just leave Lauren alone."

"Of course," Marshall said. He guided Lauren over to the Mustang and helped her into the backseat.

Marshall climbed into the passenger seat as Kelly walked around the car. She opened the driver's-side door and got in slowly, keeping her eyes on Marshall.

"Good girl," Marshall said. He flashed a smile that was just as bright as it had been the day before. "Now drive."

Kelly had to adjust the seat so her feet could reach the pedals. She started the car and made a slow turn through the parking lot. As they passed the door to the station, she saw something on the floor just inside.

She couldn't be sure what it was, but she thought it was a body.

Kelly pulled away from the station. She flipped on her signal and headed for the ramp back to the interstate.

"No," Marshall said. "Stay on this road."

Kelly looked at the road ahead. It stretched out into the distance, running straight as an arrow between fields of black dirt. "Where does this road go?" she asked.

"Does it matter?" Marshall asked.

# SIX

They stayed on the road for hours. There were very few trees, and the road seemed to stretch on forever. After a few miles the patchy blacktop gave way to rutted gravel. Clouds of pale dust followed the car as Kelly drove past barns and farmhouses separated by miles of empty fields. In some places herds of cattle looked up as they passed, but in most there was only the black earth.

For the first hour of that long bumpy ride, very little was said. Lauren's soft crying turned to silence, and when Kelly glanced in the rearview mirror, it appeared that Lauren had fallen asleep. She couldn't tell if it was a normal sleep or something like shock.

Marshall spent a few minutes looking over

the map. After that, he just stared at the gravel road ahead with single-minded intensity.

Finally boredom overcame Kelly's fear. "Can I turn on the radio?" she asked.

"Go ahead," Marshall said.

Kelly twisted the knob and got only a burst of static. She searched through the FM channels and found nothing but distant whispers. The AM band wasn't much better, but she found a religious station near the bottom of the dial. The voice of a country preacher boomed through the car for a few seconds.

Then Marshall put his hand over Kelly's and turned it off. "I can't take that stuff," he said.

A smart response came quickly to Kelly's tongue, but fear pushed it back. "Where are we going?" she asked.

"You'll see when we get there."

"Well, wherever it is, we're going to have to find a gas station soon. This car drinks a lot of gas."

"You let me worry about that," Marshall said.

Kelly risked a look at him and was surprised to see that he looked pale and nervous. "What are you going to do with us?" she asked.

"That depends on you," he said. "As long as you do what I say, you'll be fine."

Kelly swallowed. She didn't know if it was

72

better to keep him talking or leave him alone—high school hadn't included a course in dealing with maniacs. But every mile that they traveled down this desolate road was another mile away from the route where they were supposed to be. Every minute decreased the chance that anyone looking for them would ever find them.

"You killed someone back there, didn't you?" she said. She was surprised by the strength in her own voice.

"What do you think happened?" Marshall asked.

"I think you shot the station attendant," Kelly said. She stopped to lick her dry lips before going on. "I guess you were going to steal his car, or maybe you wanted the money. Anyway, we came back and Lauren saw everything."

"You're a very smart girl, Kelly." He stretched out an arm and put his hand on the back of her seat. "I can't say I'm sorry you came back. You girls have been a big help to me."

Kelly leaned forward to keep from touching his hand. "Why did you pick us in the first place?"

"That was really a great piece of luck. If you hadn't come along when you did, well, I could have been in a very tight spot."

"You were running," Kelly guessed. "When

we picked you up, I mean. You were running away from some crime."

"Let's just say I was in quite a hurry to do some traveling." He laughed, not the gentle chuckle he had used when joking with Lauren, but a mean, hard-edged laugh.

In the backseat Lauren moaned and mumbled something in her sleep. Kelly glanced at her in the mirror. She knew there was something wrong about the way Lauren was reacting, but she didn't know if waking her or letting her sleep was better.

Kelly looked over at Marshall and saw that his blue eyes were again touched with that frightening inner fire. "When you don't need us anymore, you'll kill us. Won't you?" she asked.

"Like I said," Marshall replied, "that depends on you."

"They're going to catch you," Kelly said.

Marshall snatched his hand back from her chair. "They won't catch me."

"You were going to ride with us all the way to Denver, but then you changed your mind. Why did you change your mind, Marshall? Did the police know where you were going?"

"We've talked enough," he said.

"They probably found your car."

"Shut up."

"I wonder if they've found that gas-station attendant yet?"

74

"That's enough!" For the first time his voice rose with anger. "You girls are useful, but if you get in my way, I'll leave you lying in a ditch. You understand?"

Kelly nodded. That was the end of the conversation.

It was well after noon and the gas gauge was almost at E before the road intersected a larger highway. "Which way?" Kelly asked.

"Turn left," Marshall replied.

A few minutes later Kelly saw a water tower standing above the plains. And not long after that she saw a small town at its base. "Just in time," she said.

"Turn in over there," Marshall said. He pointed to a store at the edge of the town. It had a row of gas pumps and a glass front that showed shelves of groceries inside.

Kelly pulled up next to one of the pumps. "Now what?"

"Fill it up, and get a six-pack of soda. If it were your friend here," he jerked his thumb at Lauren, "I'd have her get me something stronger. But I don't think they'd sell it to you."

"What about something to eat?"

"Get whatever you want. You have cash?" Marshall asked.

"Yes."

"Good, use it. Don't use a credit card."

"Okay," Kelly said. She opened her door and started to get out.

Marshall put a hand on her arm. "And remember, I'm right out here watching. You do anything I don't like—anything—and I'll make sure that pretty Lauren never wakes up."

Kelly had thought that she had run out of fear, but at his words her stomach tightened. "All right," she said.

"One more thing," he said. "Buy some shoelaces, the kind for sneakers. Get at least four pairs."

"Shoelaces," Kelly repeated numbly.

"Don't forget." Marshall eased the gun from his satchel. "I'd hate to have to use this."

Kelly closed the door and walked around the car to pump the gas. She hadn't noticed how her hands were shaking until she tried to get the nozzle into the gas tank. It took her three tries, and she spilled a puddle of gas beside the car. She could feel Marshall's eyes on her all the time.

When the tank was full, she wrestled the hose back onto the pump. Her hands were burning from the spilled gas, and she wished she could go to the bathroom and wash them off, but she was sure that Marshall wouldn't allow it. She settled for wiping her hands on her jeans and walked toward the store.

A cowbell over the door clanked as Kelly walked in, and the woman behind the counter looked up with a smile. She was an older lady, with short gray hair and thick metal-rimmed glasses. "Good afternoon," she said.

Kelly opened her mouth to answer, then remembered that Marshall was watching. She turned away from the counter and walked back between the racks of food. She snatched a bag of nacho chips from one rack. It wasn't what she wanted—she hated food like that—but it would have to do. She walked back to the refrigerated cases. There didn't seem to be any six-packs, so Kelly pulled out individual cans. The heap of cans made a cold clumsy bundle in her arms, and she hurried toward the counter to put them down.

"Is this everything?" the woman asked.

"Yes," Kelly said. "Wait, I mean no." She looked out the window and saw Marshall looking in. "Just a minute."

She backed away from the counter and went to find the shoelaces. She found car supplies, magazines, and toiletries, but no shoelaces. She went back to the counter and asked for them, aware every moment that Marshall might think she was saying something about him.

The woman pursed her lips and craned her neck as she peered around the store. "I know we have some. Hmmm . . . oh yes! They're right back there in the corner, beside the fishing lures."

"Thank you," Kelly said. She fought back a wave of hysterical laughter. Beside the fishing lures. Of course!

The laces were on a rack that separated them by size and type, but almost all of the slots in the rack were empty. All that remained were short black laces and long leather bootlaces. There were no sneaker laces.

Kelly grabbed the bootlaces. How many had Marshall asked for? She couldn't remember. There were six pairs. She took them all. When she turned to go back to the counter, a policeman was standing at the entrance to the store.

Like the woman behind the counter, the policeman had a head of shining silver hair. A matching gray mustache hung over his mouth. His uniform was tan, with a bright silver star that peeked through the open front of a worn leather jacket. When she saw him, the relief that went through Kelly was so strong that she almost fell. One of the packages of bootlaces dropped from her hands and clicked on the wooden floor. She didn't notice.

Everything's going to be all right. The police are here, and they'll take care of everything.

78

Kelly felt an unstoppable smile come to her face.

The policeman was looking at her curiously as she walked toward him. "You need something, miss?" he asked.

"Yes," Kelly breathed.

She was almost to him, the big grin still frozen on her face, when she remembered that Marshall was watching. Marshall was sitting outside with the barrel of his pistol against Lauren's sleeping head.

"What's wrong?" the policeman asked.

"Nothing's wrong," Kelly said quickly. She cursed herself for being so stupid. If Marshall even thought she had said something, he could be angry enough to kill Lauren. "I just wanted to know how far it is to Kansas City."

The policeman exchanged a puzzled look with the woman at the counter. "Child, if you're going to Kansas City, you're going the wrong way."

"I probably got things mixed up," she said. She dropped the packs of bootlaces on the counter. "That's all I need."

The woman pushed her glasses up with one finger. "You got gas, didn't you?"

"That's right."

The woman slowly worked the keys on her cash register. All the while the policeman stood at the end of the counter. "You're sure you're all right?" he asked.

*I'm being kidnapped*, she thought. But what she said was, "Yes, I'm fine." She added what she hoped was a reassuring smile.

The woman gave Kelly the total and put all her purchases in a paper sack. Kelly paid her and picked up the bag.

"Can I help you with that?" the policeman asked.

Kelly shook her head. She didn't trust herself to say another word without blurting out the whole story. She hurried out to the car and climbed in. Lauren was still asleep in the backseat.

Marshall took the sack from her and put it at his feet. "Drive," he demanded.

Kelly drove. In minutes only the water tower marked the location of the little town on the wide prairie behind them. The highway ended at a T intersection. Kelly stopped. The road in front of them was blacktopped and lined by telephone poles.

"Which way now?"

"What did you say to the policeman?" Marshall asked.

"Nothing," Kelly said. The pain was so sudden and intense that it took Kelly a moment to realize that he had slapped her.

"What did you say to the policeman?"

"He asked me if I needed anything."

"Yes?"

"And I told him no," she said.

"And that's all?" he asked mildly.

"That's all."

Marshall took her chin in his hand and turned her face toward him. "Kelly, Kelly. Don't lie to me. You said more than that, and so did he."

"I said yes." Her words were blurred by his hand on her face. "I asked him directions to Kansas City, and he told me I was going the wrong way."

"And then?"

"Nothing. I mean, that's all."

"You're sure?" he said.

"Yes."

Marshall released her chin. "Turn left again. And the next time I send you into someplace, don't talk to anyone. Is that clear?"

Kelly nodded, but his words hurt as much as the slap. *The next time*, he had said. How many times would she have to repeat this act? How long would this nightmare go on? There was a pain in her throat as sobs struggled to get out. It had been hours since she had eaten, but fear filled her like a lump of iron.

She drove the Mustang up onto the black-top. Gravel spun away from the tires as she accelerated. Driving on the smooth road seemed amazingly quiet after the hours they had spent rumbling across gravel.

There was a gentle rise ahead, and as they reached the top, a green sign went by on the right. WELCOME TO NEBRASKA, read the sign.

"Well, what do you know, Toto," Marshall said. "We're not in Kansas anymore." His laugh echoed in the car.

# SEVEN

From the sun and the few highway signs she saw, Kelly figured they spent most of the afternoon going north. This road wasn't quite as desolate as the one they had followed across Kansas. They passed through several small towns, where there was more traffic. Lauren slept the entire time, and Kelly began to wonder if she would ever wake up. When sunset came, they were rolling though one of a series of small ranching communities.

"We'll have to stop soon," Marshall announced.

"Already?" Kelly asked.

"I don't want you to drive when you're tired," he said. "I can't afford an accident. And Lauren's in no condition to drive." Marshall pointed at a sign beside the road that advertised a motel some miles ahead. "We'll stay there tonight."

"Why don't you drive?" Kelly asked.

"Don't be stupid," Marshall replied. "It's too hard to drive and hold a gun at the same time."

"Oh." She glanced down at his rough hands on the knees of his jeans and the brown satchel resting in his lap. "I guess that's true."

The sunset was beautiful. A thousand shades of purple poured across the sky, and the western horizon glowed with crimson light for long minutes. It seemed wrong to Kelly that anything could look so nice when she was so terrified.

Then it was dark. There was no period of getting dark. It just was dark. And the black sky was filled with ten times the number of stars that Kelly could see from home.

A grayish form ran through the headlights and disappeared into the scrub at the side of the road. "What was that?" Kelly asked.

"Coyote," Marshall said. "There are lots of them around here."

Kelly glanced over at him. "Are you from around here, Marshall?"

"No," he said. "I'm not from anywhere."

"But you're not a medical student from Indiana, either. Are you?"

"As far as you're concerned, I am."

The motel turned out to be a small place where the rooms were little buildings set off by themselves. At one time it might have been charming. Now it looked run-down and shabby.

"Are you sure we should stay here?" Kelly asked.

"I've stayed in worse," Marshall said. He reached over and turned off the engine. "Go get us a room, and remember to pay with cash."

"What should I tell them?" she asked.

"About what?"

"About us. Who do I say we are?"

Marshall snorted. "Tell them anything you want. Tell them we're brother and sister. Tell them that we're married. Tell them that we're not married. I don't think the folks that run this place are going to care."

Marshall was right. The guy behind the motel counter wore a stained white T-shirt that was barely big enough to cover his bulging stomach. Kelly just asked for a room, and he gave it to her with no questions asked. For twenty-four dollars he handed over the keys to one of the little bungalows.

When she got back outside, Marshall was helping Lauren out of the car. Lauren still seemed half asleep, but Kelly was glad to see her standing up.

"Give me the keys," Marshall said. He took

the plastic key ring from Kelly and shoved it in his jeans. "Now help me get her to the room. She's still pretty out of it."

Kelly positioned herself on one side of Lauren, holding on to her right arm while her left was draped over Marshall's shoulders. Lauren stumbled forward with her head hanging down. Her eyes were open but unfocused.

"What's wrong with her?" Kelly asked. "Shouldn't she have snapped out of this by now?"

Marshall grunted as he took most of Lauren's weight. "How should I know?"

"Aren't you the medical student?"

"Shut up," he replied.

Marshall slipped as he tried to open the door to the room, and Lauren almost fell. Kelly strained to hold her up until Marshall could steady her again. Lauren's face lay on Kelly's shoulder, looking terribly slack and empty.

"She'd better be okay," Kelly said.

Marshall paused with his hand on the doorknob. "What was that?"

"Lauren better be okay, or I'll—"

"You'll what?" Marshall interrupted. At the sound of his voice, the anger that had been building in Kelly turned to fear. He leaned toward her, the limp form of Lauren the only thing between them. "Never threaten me," he said. He pushed open the door, and together they managed to get Lauren inside.

The heat wasn't on in the little cabin, and it was just as cold inside as out. The air smelled of old cigarettes and mildew. The two beds were narrow and covered with yellow blankets so faded they were almost white. There was a small round table with an ancient black phone at one end of the room and a green-painted dresser at the other. Only the television looked new.

"Charming," Marshall said. He eased Lauren onto one of the beds, and the old mattress squeaked and sagged.

He walked across the room and picked up the telephone. "They should charge extra for the antiques," he said. Then he gave the phone a savage yank. The cord came out of the wall with a little explosion of plaster dust. "Wouldn't want you to get tempted."

Kelly didn't mind. It had just occurred to her that Marshall meant to sleep. And if he slept, that would be their chance. All she had to do was hit him or maybe take the gun away. She was so caught up in this idea that she barely heard Marshall talking to her.

"What was that?"

"I asked you where the shoelaces were," he said.

"Oh, I left those in the car," she said.

"Go get them. I'll stay here and take care of your little friend." He ran a hand over Lauren's slack cheek. "Don't leave us alone too long."

Kelly hurried across the gravel to the car. The thought of what Marshall might do to the sleeping Lauren was enough to make her almost run. She knocked on the door and sweated every second until Marshall opened it.

"Here they are." She handed him the sack.

Marshall took out a package and looked at them. "I thought I said sneaker laces."

"They didn't have any."

"I suppose these will do." He looked up at Kelly. "If you need to do anything to get ready for bed, then do it now. You won't get another chance."

"I think I'll just keep my jeans on," Kelly said.

Marshall laughed. "Always a good idea. Okay then, lie down next to Lauren."

"Lie down? But there's not enough room on these beds."

"Fine. You can always sleep on the other bed with me."

Kelly sat down on the bed beside Lauren and took off her shoes. She watched as Marshall unwrapped the package and stretched the leather laces to their full length. And then she understood what she should have known since he first asked her to pick up the laces. Understood why Marshall wasn't worried about going to sleep. "You're going to use those to tie me up, right?"

"Yes," he said. "Put your feet together." He knelt in front of her with a pair of laces in his hand. "Don't get any bright ideas," he added.

Kelly shivered at the feel of his hands on her feet and the rough strands of leather sliding around her ankles. She tried to keep a small gap between her feet, to make some slack she might use to escape, but Marshall pushed her feet back together, binding them firmly.

"That's too tight," she said.

"It's your fault for getting leather laces," he replied. "They'll stretch, so I have to make them extra tight to begin with."

He stood up and held out another bootlace. "Now your hands."

Kelly was closer to crying than she had been since Lauren had come stumbling out of the gas station. It was hard to believe that it had only been that morning, that the whole long ordeal had lasted less than twenty-four hours. And two nights before, Kelly had gone to sleep in her own bed, dreaming of the great vacation to come. She closed her eyes to hold back the tears.

Marshall pulled Kelly's hands behind her back and lashed them together. He tugged the leather laces tight, and they bit into Kelly's wrist. "I could tie you to the bed," he said thoughtfully. "But I don't think that's necessary. You aren't going to go anywhere, are you?"

"No," she whispered.

Marshall leaned over her, and again his mask of charm slipped. The expression on his face wasn't a smile—it was a leer. "Seeing you like this is very tempting." He ran a hand through her hair and cradled her neck.

He lifted her from the bed until her face was only an inch from his. "You know, we could have a real good time together. I don't think Lauren will mind."

Kelly closed her eyes again. "Leave me alone," she choked out.

Marshall pulled his hand away and let her fall back to the bed. "Your friend is prettier anyway."

Kelly opened one eye and watched as Marshall started to tie up Lauren's feet. He looked up at her. "Maybe Lauren and me will have some fun before she even wakes up."

Lauren's foot came up and struck him in the face.

Marshall flew backward and fell across the dresser. Lauren surged to her feet and went toward him. Kelly strained against her bonds, but she could do nothing but watch.

90

Marshall rolled over and looked up with an emotion Kelly could have sworn was fear. Lauren was standing over him. The brown satchel that held his gun was on the other bed. She could surely beat him to it. Or she could kick him or . . . but it didn't matter, because Lauren wasn't really awake.

She was batting at the air in front of her; waving her arms as if she was fighting off cobwebs. Her eyes darted around the room, following things that Kelly couldn't see.

Marshall chuckled and stood up. Lauren's eyes danced across him unseeing. He grabbed her wrists. "It's all right, Lauren. Go back to bed." She struggled for a second longer; then she sagged against him. Marshall half carried her back to the bed and put her beside Kelly. She didn't stir again while he bound her feet and hands.

"Now," Marshall said, "if you'll be quiet, that's all it will take. If you start making any noise, I'll have to gag you. Understand?"

"Yes," Kelly said.

"Then I'm going to bed. You better hide your eyes if you don't want to see something, little girl." Marshall pulled off his shirt, revealing a body that was flat and hard. His hands went to the buckle of his jeans and Kelly looked away. A moment later she heard him slide into bed.

91

"When will you let us go?" she asked.

"When we get where we're going."

"Where are we going?"

"You don't need to know that," Marshall said. "Now go to sleep."

Kelly lay awake for a long time. Lauren seemed to be sleeping peacefully again, and after a while Kelly heard Marshall's breathing change to a slow, even rhythm. But Kelly was afraid to sleep. She was half afraid of what Marshall might do if he woke up first. And she was afraid of the dreams that might come. But when at last she did sleep, it was only darkness.

It was the shower that woke Kelly up. She rolled over and saw Lauren beside her, but Marshall's bed was empty. Kelly tried to sit up—a hard thing to do with her hands tied behind her back. Listening carefully to the sounds of the shower, she pushed herself off the end of the bed.

She felt like a human pogo stick as she hopped across the floor. Twice she fell to her knees and had to roll over before she could stand up again. But at last she reached her goal—the old green dresser. She knelt down, turned her back to the dresser, and worked the drawer open with her free fingers. Then she turned around and looked inside. There was only a thin blanket and a battered copy of the Gideon's Bible.

Kelly pushed the drawer closed with her legs and repeated the trick on the other three drawers in the dresser. They were all empty. Kelly slumped down. Her arms and legs ached from the effort of working against the knots Marshall had tied. She put her back against the wall and pushed her way to her feet. She was going to get back on the bed when she noticed there was a drawer in the small table that the phone sat on. She started hopping toward it.

The shower went off and Kelly froze. She looked at the bathroom door, then back at table. She bit her lip and kept going. She was almost there when she heard the shower curtain being pulled back. Kelly turned so she could open the drawer. Her fingers slid off the slick wood for a few frustrating seconds before she got a grip and it slipped open. She turned, sure that she was going to be disappointed again.

There was a pen, some stationery, and a stack of envelopes in the drawer. Kelly twisted around again and stretched her fingers down to grasp the pen. She couldn't get a grip on the stationery, but she managed a hold on one of the envelopes.

There was another noise from the bathroom. Kelly turned, knocked the drawer closed with her knee, and bounded toward the bed. The mattress was still bouncing from her impact when the bathroom door opened and Marshall came out.

He wore his jeans, and a ragged towel was over his shoulders. His dark hair was wet, and drops of water clung to his skin. "Good morning," he said.

Kelly worked her fingers behind her to slide the envelope and pen into her jeans. "I need to go to the bathroom," she said.

"Sure. I don't think you can get into any trouble in there." Marshall walked over and pulled her up. "Be good while I untie you, or you'll have to hop in there."

"Okay."

He set to work on the knots on her ankles. Kelly thought about trying to kick him like Lauren had, but she was sure that he was ready for that. Marshall had been right that the leather would stretch. The laces weren't nearly as painful as when he had first tied her. Still, she could feel blood rushing into her feet when he unraveled the last knot. She turned so he could get to her hands.

Kelly was afraid that he would spot the pen jutting from the back of her jeans, but he untied her hands without a word. "Thank you," she said as she massaged her aching hands.

"Just don't take too long in there," Marshall said.

She nodded and slipped past him. She shut the bathroom door, locked it, and leaned against it. Just having the barrier between herself and Marshall felt very good.

As soon as she slid the pen and envelope from her pocket, she had her doubts. The envelope was so old it had turned yellow. The pen looked just as ancient. It would be just perfect if she had done all of this only to find that the pen wouldn't write.

It wrote.

*Kidnapped*, Kelly wrote. *Kelly Tallon and Lauren Miki from St. Louis. Being held by a man with blue eyes and dark-brown hair who calls himself Marshall. Traveling north in a blue Mustang with Missouri plates.* She wished she could remember Lauren's license-plate number, or if Marshall had given a last name after they had picked him up. But she hoped what was on the note would be enough.

She looked around the bathroom for somewhere to hide the note. She wanted to put it someplace where Marshall wouldn't see it if he came back in the room, but where whoever came to clean up when they were gone would be bound to find it. Her first thought was the shower, but then she had a better idea.

Just above the sink was a light fixture that held a single bulb. Being careful not to make noise, Kelly removed the cover. The bulb was hot, but she managed to turn it enough to make it go out. With the light out it was pitch-black in the bathroom, but she managed to get the envelope into the lamp and the cover back on.

"You almost done in there?"

"Yes," Kelly called. "Just a minute."

When she came out, Kelly was startled to see Lauren sitting on the side of the bed talking with Marshall.

"Look who's up," Marshall said.

"Lauren, are you okay?"

"Sure, Kel, but . . . well, I just don't understand how we got here." Lauren smiled apologetically. "I don't know what's wrong with me."

Kelly walked over to Lauren. "What do you remember?"

"I remember getting to the motel, getting up to see . . . the rest of the night. But I just don't remember yesterday at all."

"I was telling her about the shortcut we were taking," Marshall said, "and how we got lost." He gave a little laugh. "I can understand why she doesn't want to remember that."

"But, Lauren, don't you remember the gas station?" Kelly asked.

"Gas station?" Lauren looked genuinely puzzled.

Marshall stepped between them. "Look, let

me get my stuff and we'll go find a place to eat. We can talk about it there." He walked around the corner into the bathroom.

Kelly heard him flip the light switch several times. "It's burned out," she called.

"What gas station?" Lauren repeated.

"Lauren!" Kelly whispered fiercely. "We didn't get lost, Marshall kidnapped us. Don't you remember anything?"

"Kidnapped?" Lauren said. "That's not funny, Kel."

Marshall came out of the bathroom. "Are we ready to go?"

"Yes," Lauren said. "I think so."

"Good. Then let's get out of this dump." Marshall held the door while Lauren went out. After she left, he turned to Kelly. "And you watch what you say."

She left the room and followed Lauren across the gravel parking lot.

# EIGHT

Kelly wanted to scream. Not out of fear of Marshall, but out of pure frustration.

She had gone through the confusion and sudden terror of the gas station. Had suffered through the long drive filled with a mixture of fear and boredom. Had fought off panic back at the grocery store. Had submitted to being tied up with the leather strips while Marshall leered over her. And now, here was Lauren, talking and laughing with Marshall as if nothing had happened.

"I'm really sorry I'm acting so weird," Lauren said as Kelly walked up. "I don't know why I can't remember anything." She ran a hand over her short hair.

"It's all right," Marshall said. "It could be just some stress you're under."

"Or a shock," Kelly suggested.

Lauren turned to her. "What kind of shock?"

Behind Lauren's back Marshall was shaking his head and making suggestive gestures with the brown satchel that held his pistol. But Kelly was too upset to stop herself.

"Like being kidnapped and dragged across two states," she said.

Marshall laughed. "Sounds like Kelly must be having some trouble with her memory, too."

Lauren was looking at Kelly with a strange expression. She tilted her head to one side, and her forehead creased in confusion. "Why do you keep saying that, Kel?"

"Because it's true," Kelly said firmly.

Marshall sighed loudly. "Well, I guess I better explain what happened yesterday." He put his hands in his pockets and leaned back against the car. "You know that Kelly didn't want me riding along with you, right?"

Lauren nodded.

"Well," he continued, "she tried to get me to stay at that place we were at yesterday until a friend could come and get me."

"That's not true!" Kelly shouted, but she could see how much Marshall was enjoying this; how fooling Lauren had become another part of his game.

"You and Kelly fought," he said, and the expression on his face was a fine imitation of regret. "Believe me, I'm sorry about it. I never wanted to step between two friends like you."

"Liar," Kelly said.

Lauren hushed her. "Let him finish," she said.

"Anyway," Marshall said, "you told her you were going to help me, and we decided to get off the interstate and see some scenery along the way." He shrugged. "We got lost, and here we are."

"That's not the way it happened," Kelly said.

Lauren put both hands over her face and shook her head. "I just can't remember."

Marshall put a gentle hand on her shoulder. "It'll come back to you," he said. His voice was as kind as it had ever been, but over her lowered head, he was flashing Kelly a look of pure hate. "Do you feel up to driving?"

"Yes," Lauren said. She nodded her head and pulled her hands away. "Let's get on the road, okay?"

Marshall opened the door and helped Lauren into her seat. "Don't worry," he told her. "It'll be all right." He shut the door with a solid thump.

Kelly started to get in on the other side, but Marshall took her arm in a painfully tight grip. "You say one more word about what happened yesterday and I'll snap your little neck. We'll see

101

how pretty Lauren reacts to that shock."

"You're sick," Kelly said. Her voice was trembling, but she hadn't cried yet, and she wasn't going to give Marshall that satisfaction now. "You're enjoying this."

"It helps to pass the time," Marshall said. He opened the door and pushed the front seat down so Kelly could get in the back.

A few miles up the road there was a town large enough to support a cluster of fast-food places. Marshall and Lauren picked a place and slid into the drive-thru lane. Kelly didn't want to ask for anything, didn't want to talk to either one of them. But she hadn't eaten much over the last two days, and she was getting very hungry. She gave her order as quickly as she could.

Marshall was keeping up the pretense that they had been lost the day before, and he consulted the map while they munched their food in the parking lot. "We could turn around and take this road back the way we came," he said, "but it'll take us all day and we'll still be a long way from where we need to go."

"Is there another way?"

Marshall pointed at the thin lines that wandered over the map. "If we stay on this road, it'll lead us to this other interstate. From there we can go west to Denver."

Kelly peered through the gap between the

front seats. "It looks to me like that interstate runs northwest."

"We'll have to turn south once we're in Wyoming, but it should be a lot faster than going back."

"All right," Lauren said. "Let's get going."

The landscape began to change from that of midwestern farms to the high plains. The plowed fields of dark earth gave way to gently rolling hills covered in sparse grass and brush. There were cows, but they were strung out in small clumps instead of tightly packed herds. Outside of the towns, the houses were even farther apart, and for miles they drove between hills where not a single building was visible.

Kelly was cold in the backseat. There had been frost on the car when they started out that morning, and if the heat was on in the front, none of it had worked its way back to Kelly. She curled into a ball, wishing she had never left home.

Marshall and Lauren carried on a conversation through most of the morning. Kelly didn't pay much attention to what they were saying. It seemed like the same conversation they had been having the night they picked up Marshall: Lauren's dad drove her too hard, the guys in high school never treated her like a person, why shouldn't she go to the school where she wanted to go? Marshall nodded and made agreeable noises to everything she said. Every now and then Marshall interjected some little story of his own that backed up what Lauren was saying.

Then Lauren suddenly stopped talking. She relaxed her foot on the gas pedal, and the car began to slow.

"What's wrong?" Marshall asked.

She looked over at him. "Didn't you say you weren't going to ride with us today?"

"No, I . . ."

Kelly leaned close. "It was yesterday. He said that about yesterday."

Lauren nodded. "You wanted us to take you somewhere. Then you were going to get a ride with someone else."

Marshall was shaking his head hard. "It never happened, Lauren. You must have dreamed it."

But Lauren didn't even seem to hear him. "We took you to—"

"A gas station!" Kelly shouted.

"Yes," Lauren said. "That's right, to a gas station."

"No," Marshall said. "It never happened."

"We dropped him off," Kelly prompted.

"And then I went back for a soda," Lauren said. She was nodding her head enthusiastically now. "I remember!"

"Lauren, stop this!" Marshall practically shouted.

"I went in for a soda, and I saw Marshall standing beside the counter and he had a . . ." She stumbled for a second, and Kelly saw her stiffen. "He had a gun in his hand and there was a—"

Lauren slammed on the brakes.

Kelly was thrown against the back of Lauren's seat. The force of the impact knocked the breath out of her, and she could see the landscape outside the car revolving like the view from a merry-go-round as the car went spinning down the highway.

The horn sounded as Lauren was pushed against the wheel, but she had her seat belt on. She fought with the car, trying to keep it from sliding into a ditch, but never letting the pressure off the brakes.

Marshall was not wearing his seat belt. His head struck the windshield hard enough to leave a star of cracks in the tinted glass. He bounced back, and Kelly got a glimpse of his dark-blue eyes rolling back as he slumped and slid down in his seat.

The Mustang slid around one last time, tottered on two wheels as if it might roll over, then fell back to the pavement and was still. For a few seconds Kelly was aware of nothing but her own painful effort to pull air into her bruised chest. Then the door opened, the seat in front of her flopped down, and Lauren was leaning over her.

"Are you okay, Kel?" she asked anxiously.

Kelly nodded. "Marshall," she choked out. "What about Marshall?"

Lauren looked over at the other seat and then back at Kelly. "He looks out of it. I think he hit his head."

Kelly nodded again, and she held her hands out. Lauren helped her climb out of the car. Standing up, Kelly felt better, and her labored breathing was easier.

Lauren was looking through the open door at Marshall's crumpled form. "You don't think he's dead, do you?"

"No," Kelly managed. "I don't think so."

"Oh, Kel. You were right, weren't you? He kidnapped us." She turned to Kelly and her eyes were very bright, brimming with tears. "I'm sorry I didn't listen to you."

Everything got blurry. It took Kelly a moment to realize it was because she was crying herself. "It's okay."

Lauren held out her arms, and for a long minute the two friends stood beside the road and hugged each other while a chill wind whistled around the stopped car.

"What do we do now?" Lauren said at last.

"We go to the police," Kelly said. "I think he killed more people than the one at the gas station."

"You think he'll stay out long enough for us to get somewhere with a police station?"

"I'm not taking a chance on that." Kelly walked around to the passenger side of the car and opened the door. "Come on, help me."

Lauren walked around to join her. "What are you going to do?"

"We'll leave him here. Then we don't have to worry about finding help before he wakes up."

Kelly reached in and grabbed one of Marshall's arms. She half expected him to suddenly spring up and grab her, but his arm was as limp as a rag doll's. It took all their strength to pull Marshall out of the car and into the lank grass at the side of the road. His forehead was swollen terrifically.

"Now what?" Lauren asked.

"Now we tie him up like he did to us."

"He tied us up?"

Kelly took Lauren's wrist and held it up to her face. "Look."

Lauren stared at the thin red lines where the tight leather strips had worked into her skin. "That jerk," she said fiercely.

Kelly spotted Marshall's brown satchel lying

on the floor of the car. She reached for it and pulled it out. "We need the shoelaces he used on us. Let's see if he's got them in here." She opened the satchel and started to look inside. She could see the dull metal gleam of the pistol, a roll of money, and what looked like several yellow plastic pill bottles.

Marshall groaned and rolled over.

"Kelly, come on, let's go."

"He's not tied up," Kelly said. "He might just get up and walk away."

Marshall moaned again. Lauren took several steps away from him. "Where can he go? It's been ten miles since we even saw a house. And at least we'll be away from him."

"Okay," Kelly said. She closed the satchel and tossed it back into the car. "Let's get out of here."

Lauren practically ran around the car and jumped into her seat. As Kelly was shutting her door, Marshall got his hands under him and pushed himself to his knees. By the time the car cleared the next hill, Marshall was on his feet and staggering after them.

"That was close," Lauren said. "Is the gun in the bag?"

"Yeah."

"We should have just shot him."

Kelly looked at her, trying to see if she was

serious. Lauren looked serious. "The police will get him," Kelly said.

A red pickup truck came toward them in the left lane. "Maybe we can get them to help us," Lauren suggested, pointing at the truck.

"It's probably just an old farmer or something. We better wait till we can find somebody that knows what they're doing." The truck rolled past on the left, and Kelly got a glimpse of a man in a cowboy hat. Kelly turned to watch the truck as it disappeared into the distance. Watching it pass out of sight, she suddenly felt very light-headed. "We made it," she said. "We got away from him."

They drove on for a few minutes before coming to a store on the side of the road. Even from a distance, it was obvious that the store had been closed for a very long time. But there was a bright blue sign at its side and a telephone booth that looked like it was still in business.

"Let's pull over there," Kelly said. "We can call the police before he has a chance to get away."

Lauren pulled off into the dirt parking lot. Both girls got out of the car and walked over to the booth. It was one of the old kind, a little metal-and-glass room with a folding door on one side. "Which one of us should call?" Lauren asked.

"I will." Kelly stepped into the booth. She picked up the phone and punched 911. Then she frowned.

"What's wrong?" Lauren asked.

"We're too far out in the country. There's no emergency system here."

"Call the operator. They'll know what to do."

It took a few minutes of question and answer for the operator to figure out which police department covered the area where they were calling from. Then Kelly had to insist that the call was a real emergency.

"What's going on?" Lauren asked.

"They're putting us through to a sheriff's office. It's ringing now." Over Lauren's shoulder Kelly saw a vehicle coming down the road in the same direction that they had come. It looked like a pickup.

"Sheriff's office," said a voice over the phone.

"Hello," Kelly said. "I want to report a murder and a kidnapping."

"Is this a joke?"

"No," Kelly said. "No joke."

"Can you hold on just minute while I get the sheriff on the line?"

"Sure." Kelly lowered the phone. "They're getting the sheriff now. It won't be long."

It was the noise that made her look up. The pickup had pulled off the road and was rumbling toward them across the parking lot.

"Miss? Are you there?" said a voice on the phone.

"Run!" Kelly shouted. She dropped the phone and ran. Lauren was just beside her as she rounded the corner of the deserted store. There was a huge crash behind them, and Kelly turned her head to see the truck—the same red pickup truck that had passed them on the road—plow through the phone both, shattering it into a thousand pieces.

"My car!" Lauren cried. "We've got to get to my car!" She turned away from the building and sprinted for the Mustang.

"No!" Kelly yelled.

But Lauren was running flat out. Brown dust puffed up around her tennis shoes as she ran. The pickup turned, and the engine roared as it started after Lauren.

Kelly ran after them, but there was nothing she could do. The truck was closing on Lauren. In a moment it would be on top of her. Then it did something that Kelly didn't expect. It swerved around Lauren, cut back in, and skidded to a stop next to the Mustang. The driver's door flew open.

Only a step away from the side of the truck,

Lauren screamed and stepped back. Kelly froze in midstep and almost fell.

Marshall stepped out of the truck.

The bump on his forehead had turned dark red. His blue eyes blazed like neon. Kelly expected him to threaten them, to strike Lauren, or to come for her. She expected to die. But none of those things happened.

Marshall stepped down out of the truck and immediately fell to his knees. He got a hand on the side of the truck and pulled himself back up. He looked at the two girls for a moment, his bright eyes sweeping over them as if he didn't recognize them. Then he walked around to the other side of the truck.

Kelly realized that she had been holding her breath since Marshall stepped out. She let her breath go in a ragged gasp and ran over to Lauren.

"Are you all right?"

Lauren shook her head. "How can I be?"

Then Kelly remembered that Marshall's satchel was in the car. "The gun!" She jumped to her feet.

Marshall came back in view around the rear of the truck. In his left hand was his small brown satchel. In his right was his gun.

"Get in the car," he said. He sounded more tired than angry. "Now." Neither girl moved.

The pistol shot was incredibly loud. The bullet kicked up a clod of hard earth from the parking lot. Kelly could feel some of it spray against the legs of her jeans. The echo of the shot bounced back and forth between the low hills.

"If I fire again," Marshall said. "It will be to kill you. Get in the car now."

Kelly gave Lauren a gentle push, and together they walked around the truck. Marshall followed close behind them with his pistol in his hand.

As she was getting in the car, Lauren stopped and looked at Kelly. "We'll never get away from him, will we?"

Kelly didn't have an answer.

# NINE

"Thanks to that little stunt," Marshall said, "we're going to have to change directions again." He seemed to be gaining strength with every mile, returning to his usual state of frightening coldness. The swelling on his forehead was going down, leaving a multicolored bruise in its place.

"Where are you trying to get to?" Kelly asked.

"Wouldn't you like to know." He turned to Lauren. "There's a highway crossing coming up in a few miles. When we get there, turn left."

"What did you do back there?" Lauren asked.

"Back there?"

"How did you get the truck?"

"Oh, the truck." Marshall leaned back in his

seat and put his feet up on the dashboard. "The truck driver was a real Good Samaritan. He stopped to see what a poor fellow was doing staggering along the roadside out in the middle of nowhere." He stopped to put a hand on Lauren's shoulder. "This trip has been full of Good Samaritans."

"What did you do to him?" Kelly asked, but she already knew the answer.

Marshall tilted his head back to look at her over the high bucket seat. "Killed him," he said calmly. "Took a piece of metal fence post out of the back of his truck and split his head open with it."

Kelly shivered, and she heard Lauren say something under her breath.

"Well, I couldn't help it, could I?" Marshall said. "You girls were off causing who-knows-what kind of trouble, and I didn't have time to reason with the man. It's your fault, really, that he's dead. I certainly wouldn't have done anything like that if you hadn't forced my hand." He put on a look that imitated regret.

Kelly wondered if any of his expressions were real or if they were all just masks to cover his complete lack of normal emotion. She didn't think that Marshall ever felt regret, and she was sure that he didn't feel guilt. This little speech was just another part of his game. Kelly didn't even think he really expected them to feel guilty about the death of the man in the cowboy hat. He only wanted to see how they would react—something to pass the time.

They reached the highway cutoff that Marshall had mentioned, and Lauren made the left turn. The new road was in worse shape than the one they had been following. Lauren had to slow down to avoid numerous potholes and sections of broken pavement. The road took them past a few new and prosperous-looking ranch houses, but more often they passed houses with faded "For Sale" signs, or houses where the roof sagged down over broken empty rooms.

They had been traveling along the bumpy road for almost an hour when they came to another small town. Like the place they had passed through the day before, this one seemed to consist only of a gas station and a grocery store.

"Kelly's turn to get us some food again," Marshall said when they stopped at the store. He got out and let Kelly escape from the backseat, reminding her not to talk to anyone or do anything that he wouldn't like. He still had the gun in his hand, and he showed it to her now. "Remember your friend," he said.

This store was larger than the other one had been. It was an older building, with regular aisles instead of small racks, and its shelves held real groceries—bread, flour, meat—not the chips and candy bars of the usual roadside places.

Kelly walked along the shelves with a grocery basket dangling from her left hand, trying to pick items that they could use along the road. She wished they had a cooler to hold some luncheon meat, some sodas. If they had brought a cooler to start with, maybe Lauren wouldn't have gone back to the gas station where Marshall had shot the clerk. Then they wouldn't be in this mess.

*Why not wish that Lauren never gave Marshall a ride in the first place?* she asked herself. She went back to selecting groceries.

She had picked up some cookies, a bag of carrots, a small bunch of bananas, and a six-pack of soda when she noticed something odd about the store. The windows didn't go all the way across. The first three aisles of the store were lined up with plate-glass windows, and anyone outside could easily see into them. But the fourth aisle, the aisle where the meat and milk sat in refrigerated cases, was hidden from the outside by a section of bare wall. And standing at the end of the fourth aisle, in the spot that was hardest to see from outside, was a clerk stacking cans on one of the wooden shelves.

Kelly glanced outside and saw that Marshall

was keeping her under close inspection. She looked away, trying to appear unaware that he was watching. With her small collection of groceries swaying in their basket, she slowly walked around the corner into the fourth aisle, out of sight of Marshall.

Her heart was pounding in her ears as she walked down the stained tile floor toward the clerk. She had to stop several times to gather her courage. The short aisle stretched out in front of her until it seemed a mile long, but at last she was there standing right behind the clerk.

She couldn't do it. It was too big a chance. She started to turn away, to forget that she had ever thought about telling someone what was going on. Then the clerk turned first.

He was a middle-aged man whose black hair was sprinkled with early gray. His face was so tanned that Kelly thought he looked more like a cowboy than a grocery clerk. "Is there something I can do for you?" he asked.

Kelly opened her mouth to speak, but no words came out. She stopped, cleared her throat, and tried again. "There's this guy," she said. The clerk looked at her patiently. "He's out in the car, and—"

"Kelly! There you are," said a voice from behind her.

Kelly felt her heart stop, felt it freeze between beats and then stutter for a moment before it picked up its hammering beat. She turned to see Marshall walking quickly down the aisle with Lauren close beside him. With the bruise on his forehead and dirt on his jeans, he looked rather ragged, but the smile on his face was as broad as ever. Lauren was smiling too, but her smile was as brittle as glass.

"We were getting worried about you," Marshall said as he got closer.

"Just getting groceries," Kelly said. There was something strange about the way Lauren was walking—she wasn't just walking beside Marshall, she was almost walking on top of him. As Marshall came up to Kelly, he slid around Lauren. He threw his arm around Kelly, and she felt the hard barrel of his pistol digging into her ribs.

"You have everything?" he asked.

"Yes," she said. "I guess so."

"Come on, then. We need to hit the road." Marshall looked at the clerk. "We're burning daylight." He jammed the gun into Kelly and steered her away from the clerk.

Marshall stayed right behind her while Kelly took her collection of groceries to the front of the store and paid for them. He exchanged a bit of pleasant conversation with the woman at the checkout, asking her about the weather and complimenting her on how nice the area was. When they got out to the car, he flipped the door opened and shoved Kelly into the back.

"That was stupid," he said as Lauren started the car. "Very stupid."

"What?" Kelly asked.

Marshall laughed. "Oh, that's good. First you act stupid, then you play stupid." His hand lashed back.

It wasn't a slap, it was a punch. Marshall's knuckles pounded into Kelly's skull just over her ear and sent her head back against the car seat. Sparks ran across her vision, and her ears rang as if a flight of bees was loose in her head.

"I didn't say anything," she said. She could see Lauren looking at Marshall in shock.

"You didn't, huh? Then what were you doing with that guy in there?"

"I was asking him where something was."

"What something?"

"Ice," Kelly said. "I thought that if we had some ice, we could keep our soda cold."

Her lie seemed to cool Marshall down a few degrees. "Maybe," he said. He turned toward Lauren. "What are you waiting for? Drive!"

The punch seem to have stunned Lauren as much or more than it had Kelly. She almost stalled the car as she left the lot, and her foot slipped off the clutch as she shifted gears, causing the transmission to growl in protest.

Despite the chilly weather, Kelly was sweating. Drops of sweat trickled over her ribs. Her hands left damp prints on the vinyl of the Mustang's rear seat. She expected Marshall to turn back to her, to hit her again, or maybe even to pull out his gun. She almost wanted him to. Anything had to be better than just letting this thing go on and on. But Marshall didn't say another word to her.

Instead Marshall seemed to be intent on making Lauren change roads. They took so many turns that Kelly thought they had to be driving in circles.

The landscape grew even more desolate. The clumps of brown grass were separated by several feet of bare, stony ground, and the fences bordering the road were rusty and dilapidated. Tumbleweeds as big as barrels went skittering across the road like careless children. They passed fields that contained nothing but row after row of knee-high anthills, and other fields where prairie dogs stood sentry over cities of dusty holes.

It was still early when Marshall announced that they were going to stop for the night. "Why so soon?" Kelly asked.

Marshall turned to her with his warm, sincere smile—the smile Kelly had grown to hate the most. "Are you that anxious to keep traveling?"

"I just want this over with."

"It'll be over soon enough," he said. He ran his hand over the still-livid bruise on his forehead. "But I'm tired tonight, and for some reason I have a headache."

"There's nothing here," Lauren said. "Are we just going to sleep in the car?"

"Be patient," Marshall said. "You'll see."

Ten minutes later the narrow road they had been following reached the interstate. After two days of weeds and tiny towns, the clutter of burger places, gas stations, and motels around the interstate junction looked like a city.

There were three motels to choose from. Marshall picked the one that looked cheapest and had Lauren pull into the lot. Lauren climbed out and flipped the seat up so Kelly could get out, but Marshall shoved the seat back down before Kelly could move.

"Not this time," he said. "I still don't know if I believe little Kelly's story about what she was saying to that guy back there in the grocery." He looked at Lauren. "This time we'll let Lauren get us a room."

Lauren looked frightened at the idea. "What do I do?" she asked.

123

"Just go ask for a room for yourself and your two cousins," Marshall said. "And remember that Kelly's health depends on you keeping your cool."

"It'll be okay, Lauren," Kelly tried to reassure her.

Lauren nodded, but she still looked very nervous as she closed the door and walked toward the motel office. Marshall watched her go. "Your friend's got a great body," he said to Kelly. "Too bad I can't say the same thing about her mind."

"Are you kidding? Lauren's grades are great. She's probably going to be a doctor or something."

"She'll never be a doctor," he replied. "She's not tough enough."

"She's plenty tough," Kelly said. "She always has been."

Marshall reached over the seat and snared Kelly's wrist. He pulled her close. "She's not as tough as you, Kelly. She's never had to face real pressure before, and when she did, she couldn't take it." His arm left Kelly's wrist and went around her back. He pulled her even closer, so close that his lips almost brushed her cheek when he talked. "I'm really starting to like you."

"I'm sorry to hear that," Kelly said, "because I don't like you one bit."

Marshall smiled. "Oh, you will. Give yourself a few more days." Then he slammed her back in the seat with stunning force. "Where's Lauren?" he said.

"She's only been gone a couple of minutes."

"She's had plenty of time to get a room." He craned his neck to see through the window of the motel office. "She's still talking to that clerk. She's telling him everything." His voice was rising in tone and volume like a teapot about to boil.

"No she's not," Kelly said.

"Yes she is!" Marshall said, nearly shrieking. "She's got no guts! She's telling him everything!" Then his voice dropped to a somber whisper, and the blue light—the killing light, Kelly thought—came on in his eyes. "Your friend has just killed you," he said. He pulled out the pistol and pointed it straight at Kelly.

She wanted to run, wanted to dive for cover and scream for help. But she didn't. She didn't move a muscle, didn't even draw a breath. Fear had turned her into a statue. Somewhere in her head, a piece of Kelly flew free. She floated above her own body, drifted across the roof of the car, and began to fly far away. She didn't want to be anywhere near the trembling red-haired girl when the man with the pistol pulled the trigger.

125

Then Lauren opened the door of the Mustang and the two halves of Kelly's mind rushed back together.

"What's going on?" Lauren asked.

Marshall kept the pistol fixed on Kelly. "Did you get a room?"

"Yes."

He lowered the pistol and smiled. "Me and Kelly were just having a little fun, right, Kel?"

Kelly fumbled out the open door, fell on her knees, and was sick on the hard blacktop of the motel parking lot.

# TEN

The leather bootlace bit into Kelly's wrist. "Ow! Do they have to be so tight this time?"

"They stretch," Marshall said. He rolled Kelly over to face the ceiling.

"I thought they'd already stretched."

"Be quiet," he said.

Lauren was beside her, also bound with the laces. Marshall hadn't stopped with tying their hands and feet. He'd also tied their legs at the knees and their arms at the elbows. He tied their hands again, wrapping the laces painfully tight.

"How long are you going to leave us like this?" Lauren asked.

"If I could trust you, I wouldn't have to do this." He leaned in close. "But I can't trust you, can I, Lauren?"

Marshall stood and walked across the room. Instead of getting ready for bed, as he'd done the night before, he pulled a comb from his little bag and stood in front of the mirror, combing back his dark hair. "Taking care of you girls is hard work. I think I deserve a night off."

"Night off?" Lauren said.

He nodded. "I'm feeling pretty thirsty. You girls won't mind if I step out and find a place to get my throat wet, will you?"

"I don't care if you drown yourself," Kelly said.

Marshall laughed. "You're so cute, Kelly. I can always count on you." He shoved the comb into the rear pocket of his jeans. "I'll be back in a while. And don't even think of trying anything."

"We'll be here," Kelly said bitterly.

He started toward the door, and then stepped back. "Oh, just one more thing." He walked across to Lauren's suitcase, which was lying on the table, and unzipped it.

"Stay out of there," Lauren said.

Marshall flipped through Lauren's clothes, throwing aside tops and flinging underwear onto the table. "I wouldn't want you two to lose your sexy voices yelling for help." He came out with two pair of rolled-up socks and walked to the bed.

128

"Don't do it," Kelly said. "We'll be quiet."

"I know you will."

"You don't have to—" Kelly started. Marshall shoved a pair of the socks into her mouth.

Immediately a cough shook her, but the wad of damp cotton in her mouth muffled everything but a thin squeak. She tried to open her jaws wider and push the socks out with her tongue, but every effort triggered a bout of choking that left her weak and struggling to breathe. Her eyes teared, and she could feel a blackness hovering over her as she fought to pull in air.

She barely heard Marshall struggling to get the socks into Lauren's mouth. He said something, but it came in the middle of a coughing fit, and Kelly only heard his mocking tone, not his words. Then she heard the door slam, and they were alone.

It took Kelly a few minutes to turn herself enough to see Lauren. When she did, she saw Lauren looking back at her. There was fury in Lauren's eyes, and her mouth was forced wide by a pair of socks.

It should have been frightening, or maddening, but the round circle of Lauren's red lips and the white tail of the socks sticking out made Kelly want to laugh. The idea that she must look just as foolish only made it seem funnier. The laughing fit triggered another bout of coughing, and again Kelly almost passed out before she could get her breathing under control.

Lauren wiggled closer. She tried to say something, but the socks made her words unintelligible. Her dark eyes bored into Kelly, trying to get the message across without words.

"What?" Kelly tried to say, but the word was only a muffled grunt.

Lauren rolled onto her side. Though her wrists were bound as tightly as Kelly's, her fingers were free. She grasped at the sleeve of Kelly's sweater and tugged hard. Then she looked back over her shoulder at Kelly.

Kelly understood what Lauren wanted. If they worked together they might be able to get free—probably could get free. But what if this was a trap?

Couldn't Marshall be testing them? He could be waiting right outside the door, listening for the sounds that would tell him they were trying to escape. And then he'd have another excuse to hit them and threaten them.

Lauren tugged at her sleeve again, more insistent this time. When she turned over, there was no mistaking the pleading in her eyes.

Kelly closed her eyes and pulled as deep a breath as she could around the mouthful of socks. Even if this wasn't a trap, was she up for it? Lauren had slept through a whole day, but

Kelly had spent that day in a pressure cooker. She wasn't sure that she had the energy to try anything. A few hours of sleep sounded almost as good as being free from Marshall.

But Lauren's fingers kept tugging, demanding attention. And at last Kelly rolled over onto her side and started worming her way down the bed.

With her legs tied together and her hands bound behind her back, it was an effort for Kelly to struggle along. Every move required her to bend and stretch like an inchworm. And with Lauren on the same bed, she had to be careful not to fall off.

The first thing she wanted out of the way was the socks in her mouth. They made it hard to communicate, and Kelly found even the thought of them disgusting.

Lauren seemed to understand what she was trying to do. As Kelly strained to slide down the bed, Lauren's fingers fumbled blindly over her face. Kelly tried to open her mouth even farther to give Lauren a better shot at the gag. She felt a tug, but the socks settled back. There was another pull, and Kelly strained her neck back. The socks slid over her teeth, and then they were out.

Kelly drew in a deep breath. "Thanks," she said. She paused for a second, relishing the ease of breathing without the gag. "What now?"

131

Lauren struggled to turn over and face Kelly. She jerked her chin upward.

Kelly frowned as she tried to puzzle out Lauren's meaning. "Come up there?"

Lauren jerked her chin upward again and made a muffled cry.

"Your gag? Take out the socks?"

Lauren nodded vigorously.

"Okay," Kelly said, "I'm coming."

It took more long minutes for Kelly to push herself back up the bed and for Lauren to get herself into position. Kelly rolled over and managed to snag the socks from Lauren's mouth— after poking her in the eye.

"I thought I was going to die," Lauren said as soon as the socks came out.

"We need to hurry," Kelly said. "Marshall could be back any minute."

"We don't need to get untied. We can just yell. Somebody's bound to hear us."

"Oh." Kelly felt uneasy about the idea, but Lauren had a point. "Hey!" she yelled. "Help!"

"In here!" Lauren cried.

They stopped for a second to listen, then yelled again. And again. And again. They yelled and screamed until their throats were raw. Lauren even twisted around so she could pound her feet against the wall. But every time they stopped, all they could hear was the sound of their own breathing.

"It's no use," Kelly said at last. "The parking lot only had a dozen cars in it. There probably isn't anybody in the rooms near us."

"So now what?" Lauren asked.

"Now we try and get our hands loose, I guess."

They went through the tedious process of getting themselves back to back and getting their hands together. For a while they both tried to work at the same time, but they got in each other's way.

"You hold still, and I'll untie you first," Kelly said. Lauren stopped moving and waited.

Kelly soon found that it wasn't as easy as she had expected. For one thing, her hands were tied squarely behind her back, and no matter how she twisted or craned her neck, she couldn't see what she was doing. For another, Marshall's knots were tight—every time Kelly tried to pull on the wrong end, Lauren gasped in pain.

After ten minutes of increasing frustration, Kelly was ready to give up. "Why don't you work on mine first?" she suggested. "I'm sure I can get you loose once my hands are untied."

But Lauren had no more luck than Kelly. By the time she stopped, Kelly's wrists were aching, and it felt as if the leather laces were buried deep in her skin.

133

They lay side by side on the bed, staring up at the water spots on the motel ceiling. "It's too bad we don't have a knife," Lauren said.

"Sure," Kelly said. "And we could also ask Marshall to leave his gun for us. I'm sure he wouldn't mind."

Lauren turned toward her, her eyes drawn into narrow slits. "Don't get sarcastic with me. If you hadn't wanted to go skiing, we wouldn't be in this mess."

"Me! Wait a minute. You're saying that this whole thing is my fault?"

"Well, you were the one who wanted to go west. I wanted to go to Florida for spring break, but—"

"Wait one minute," Kelly said. "You were the one that stopped to pick up Marshall."

"I was trying to do the right thing."

*Just leave it alone*, Kelly told herself. But her anger was building, and no matter how she wanted to hold it in, she couldn't. "Sure you were," she said. "His looks didn't have anything to do with it."

"What do you mean?" Lauren's voice was chilly.

"Come on, Lauren. You were going on and on about how great he was. I thought you were going to ask him to marry you."

"It wasn't like that. Besides, I didn't see you

134

saying anything bad about his looks."

"Yeah, but I didn't sleep with him."

As soon as the words left Kelly's mouth, Lauren stiffened. There was a painful silence, and Kelly was almost glad they were tied up. Otherwise Lauren might have slapped her.

Kelly's anger had vanished, and she wished she could take it back. But she knew that was impossible.

"I'm sorry," she said after the silence had stretched on for minutes. "I shouldn't have said that."

"How did you know?" Lauren asked softly.

"I woke up in the middle of the night and you were gone. I was worried about you."

Lauren made a strangled noise that could have been laughing or crying. Kelly could feel Lauren shaking with muffled sobs.

There was a click at the door, and both girls jerked.

"The socks," Kelly whispered. "Where are they?" Then the sound at the door turned into a rattle, and there was no time to do anything about the gags.

Marshall shoved the door open and staggered in. "Hey, how are my two babes?" Even from across the room, the smoky smell of whiskey was strong.

He slammed the door and walked over to the

bed. "I don't think I have ever seen such a good-looking pair as you two." His legs wobbled and he fell to the ground.

For a moment Kelly thought that he had passed out, but then his hands came over the edge of the bed and he pulled himself to his knees. His hair spilled down over his forehead, and his blue eyes were fuzzy and unfocused. There was a stupid smile on his lips, and for just a moment he looked like a harmless fool.

Then he reached for Kelly. He grabbed her ankle and pulled her to the edge of the bed. His face came down over hers and he kissed her with a mouth that reeked of whiskey.

Kelly twisted her face away. "Leave me alone!" she shouted.

He backed away, but the grin on his face no longer looked so harmless. "Why should I?" he said, his voice slurred by alcohol. "I've had to take care of you for days, and I'm not getting anything for it."

"Leave her alone!" Lauren said.

Marshall glanced at Lauren. "Don't be jealous, honey. I'll get back to you."

He leaned down and nuzzled his face against the base of Kelly's neck, his breath very warm on her skin. "Please stop," she cried.

"Can't stop now," he said. "Just starting to

have fun." Then he stopped and sat up halfway. "Didn't I gag you?"

"Please, just stop."

"Doesn't matter," Marshall said. "Better for kissing you this way."

He leaned in again, but before he could do anything else, he slumped against the side of the bed, asleep.

"It'll be okay," Lauren whispered. "We'll get away."

Kelly shook her head, sending a small shower of hot tears across the bed. For the first time since the nightmare had started, she gave herself over to her fear, and cried in long, aching sobs.

# ELEVEN

Kelly lay awake, staring at the ceiling as gray morning light filtered through the closed blinds. She thought about the note she had left in the last motel room. She tried to imagine someone coming into the room to clean up. They would try the bathroom light, and when they went to replace it, they would find the note. And then the police would come looking and rescue them.

Children's voices echoed from the parking lot, followed by slamming car doors, as some vacationing family started their day. Kelly lost her train of thought and looked around the room.

Lauren was asleep beside her. She had talked for an hour after Marshall had passed out, helping Kelly as much as she could.

Marshall's sleep was more troubled. Sometime in the night he had woken up enough to stumble to his own bed. He lay on top of the blankets with his arms and legs sprawled out. Every now and then he muttered something in his sleep. In between mumbling he snored. Even now his breath still smelled of stale whiskey.

Kelly hadn't slept at all. But she didn't feel tired. She felt refreshed, like her mind was working better than it had in days.

Lauren coughed and rolled over. Her eyes fluttered open, and she squinted against the gray light. "Morning," she mumbled.

"Stay quiet," Kelly whispered. "He's still asleep."

Lauren nodded.

"I don't think we're going to have many more chances."

"What . . ." Lauren started, then remembered to whisper. "What do you mean?"

"He's been making us drive north ever since he killed that guy at the gas station. I think he's heading for Canada," Kelly whispered. "And I don't think he's going to want to take us past the border guards."

Fear tightened Lauren's face. "What will he do with us?"

"I doubt he'll leave us around to tell where

he went. He'll wait until we're out on one of those side roads, in a place where there's nobody around. Then he'll take care of us."

"How long?"

Kelly would have shrugged, but lying down with her hands tied, it wasn't possible. "I don't know. Probably no more than a day or two. He's taken a big chance by keeping us around this long. Look how many times we've almost given him away."

"Why?" Lauren said. "Why keep us around if he's just going to kill us?"

"He likes the power. Everybody else that knows what he did is dead. He took us along so he'd have someone to brag to, someone to scare, someone to push around."

They were silent for a long time.

Out on the highway a big truck honked its bass horn at some obstruction. Lauren laughed under her breath.

"What?" Kelly asked.

"I was just thinking," she said, "how much better it would have been if I'd gone with that trucker instead of Marshall." She looked toward Kelly again, and though her lips were still smiling, her eyes were bright with tears.

"No!" Kelly whispered fiercely. "We're not going to cry anymore. We can't give him that." She looked across the small gap that separated

Marshall's bed from theirs. "We've got to get him before he gets us."

"You mean kill him?" Lauren asked.

"If that's what it takes."

They waited a long time for Marshall to wake up. When he finally did, he sat on the edge of the bed with his face in his hands, then stumbled into the bathroom.

"Think he's still hurting from last night?" Lauren asked.

"Yeah," Kelly replied as the sound of the shower started up in the bathroom. "Keep a close watch on him today. If he's nursing a hangover, he may not pay as much attention to us."

Marshall emerged from the bathroom with wet hair and a damp towel over his shoulders. His walk seemed more steady, but his eyes were bloodshot and his shoulders sagged. "I should have gotten more clothes out of my car when I went with you," he said as he looked at his faded flannel shirt. "I think I ought to have one of you girls run into a store and pick me up a new one."

"I want to take a shower," Kelly said.

"What?"

"A shower. We haven't had one in two days."

"A little girl as sweet as you might melt in the shower," he said, but he walked back into the bathroom for a second, then returned. "All right, there's no window in there. As long as you don't start sending Morse code with the toilet, I don't see how you can get in trouble."

He walked over to the bed and pushed Kelly onto her stomach. The knots they had tried to open the night before parted under his fingers with maddening ease. He freed her legs just as casually.

"Go take your shower," he said. "But be quick about it. I want to get moving."

"I want a shower too," Lauren said.

Marshall frowned. "If your friend here can get finished fast enough, you can have a shower too. If she takes too long, you do without."

Kelly stood up and almost fell. The leather laces had left her feet numb. She made her way to the bathroom on feet full of pins and needles, staggering even worse than Marshall had. Once inside she slammed the white door. This motel had a lock on the bathroom, and Kelly quickly turned it.

After two long days on the road, her clothes felt plastered on. She peeled them off and stepped into the shower. For the next ten minutes, she didn't think about anything but how good hot water and soap could feel.

A pounding at the door interrupted her reverie.

"If your friend is going to get a shower, you better get out now."

143

Kelly didn't want to stop. If she didn't open the door, would he break it down? No, he'd just threaten to shoot Lauren. But he couldn't do that. Not here in the motel room.

She turned off the water and stepped out of the shower. She was willing to take some chances with Marshall, but that was one risk she wasn't ready to take.

She had no choice but to put her dirty clothes back on—Marshall had carried Lauren's suitcase in to get material for his gags, but Kelly's luggage was still out in the car. She pulled on the clothes, wincing at the smell of Marshall's whiskey, which lingered on the collar of the sweater. Reluctantly she opened the bathroom door and stepped out.

"Well, there she is," Marshall said. He turned to Lauren. "All right, your turn. And don't make me have to knock twice."

Lauren hurried past with some clothes in her arms. She slammed the bathroom door behind her, and Kelly heard her fumbling at the lock. *Enjoy it while you can*, she thought.

Kelly half expected Marshall to be all over her while Lauren was in the shower, but he sat on the bed and stared off into space with his bloodshot eyes. Kelly found a brush and blow dryer in Lauren's suitcase and took them over to the counter. She flipped on the dryer and ran the brush through her damp auburn hair. Even if she couldn't have clean clothes, it made her feel a little better to have clean hair.

A hard tug on the power cord pulled the dryer from her hand. Kelly turned to see Marshall jerk the cord from the wall and throw the dryer across the room. He gave her a dull glance, then walked back over to the bed.

"Why did you do that?"

"Too loud," he said. "Use a towel."

Kelly looked around the room. There was a chair beside the dresser. Could she move fast enough to hit him with it? Where was his gun? Could she get to it first? Kelly looked at the towel in her hands. If she could get it around his neck, could she strangle him? She took a step toward Marshall, not sure what she would do, knowing only that she had to do something.

Marshall raised his head slowly and looked up at her with his deep-blue eyes. "You have a problem?"

Kelly nodded. "You."

He threw his legs off the side of the bed and sat up. "You think you can do something about it, little girl?"

With her heart pounding in her ears, Kelly nodded again. "Whatever I have to." She took another step toward him.

She never saw where the gun came from, but

suddenly it was in his hand. He pointed the weapon at her casually. "I like you, Kelly. Don't make me use this."

"You're going to kill me soon, aren't you? In only a day or two you're going to kill me and Lauren."

He stood. The hand with the gun came slowly up until the black hole of the barrel was inches from Kelly's face. Marshall might be suffering from a hangover, but it didn't show in that steady hand.

"It could be now, Kelly." His voice was cold, every word carved in ice. "Even a couple of days are better than nothing, don't you think?"

Kelly looked at the gun.

"If you cooperate," Marshall said softly, "I won't have to kill you. Now calm down before you get hurt."

She didn't believe him. Deep down she knew he still meant to kill them both. But Marshall was right about one thing: Two days were better than nothing, even two days of torture.

Kelly stepped back and turned away from him.

"Good girl," Marshall said.

Lauren came out of the bathroom a few minutes later without prompting.

"Get everything," Marshall said. "We're leaving now."

146

Kelly helped Lauren get her things back into her suitcase. Once everything was in, Lauren hefted the heavy bag and headed for the door. Kelly picked up her purse from the table. Then she glanced around and saw that Marshall was looking away. Quickly, she dropped her purse to the carpeted floor and pushed it under the dresser with the toe of her sneaker.

With Marshall following, Kelly opened the door. She was amazed to see that several inches of snow blanketed the cars and blacktop. The air that rushed into the room was bitterly cold.

"You sure we can drive in this?" Kelly asked, shivering in the doorway.

Lauren looked over her shoulder. "I don't know. I haven't got snow tires or chains."

"You can drive," Marshall snarled. "Get moving."

The wet snow chilled Kelly's feet as they hurried across the parking lot. The wind cut through her sweater and raised goose bumps on her arms. She waited while Lauren heaved her suitcase into the back of the car before speaking.

"Uh-oh," she said. "I left my purse in the room."

Marshall looked at her across the snow-covered car. "Go get it," he said, his breath making clouds of steam. "And don't get distracted or try

147

to run. One minute too long, and you and your friend will both regret it."

He tossed the key to her, and Kelly caught it out of the cold air. "Right."

She dashed back to the room and opened the door. Leaving the key dangling from the lock, she ran across the room and snatched up the phone.

Several billing options were listed on the phone. Kelly couldn't charge the call to the room, because Marshall might see the bill when they went to check out. And she couldn't take the time to ask information for the number of the local police. She quickly punched the button for the operator.

"I want to make a collect call," she said as soon as a voice came on the line. She told the operator her home phone number. "That's collect from Kelly to whoever answers."

While the phone was ringing, she plotted what she was going to say. It had to be fast—Marshall wouldn't wait for long before coming after her—and it had to contain as much information as possible: the location, Lauren's car, kidnapped, heading northwest, call the police. Whoever answered would call the police. Once they knew what had happened and where she was, Kelly was sure her parents would take care of things.

The phone clicked as someone on the other end picked up. "Hello," said Kelly's father.

"I have a collect call from Kelly," said the operator. "Will you pay—"

"There's no one available to take your call. If you'll leave your name and number at the beep, we'll get back to you as soon as possible."

"I'm sorry," the operator said. "You can try your call again later."

"Operator!" Kelly shouted. "Don't hang up."

"I can't complete the call unless someone accepts the charges."

The answering machine beeped.

"Dad! It's Kelly!"

There was a click as the connection was broken. "I am sorry," said the operator. "You can try the call later or use a convenient calling card to pay for the charges at your end."

"Sure," Kelly said. "Wait! This is an—"

There was a noise at the door. She dropped the phone back onto its cradle and walked across the room. She was just bending to get her purse when Marshall came in with his arm tight around Lauren's waist.

"Find your purse?" he asked.

"Yeah, just found it," she said. "Here it is."

Marshall threw something across the room. When it settled on one of the beds, Kelly realized that it was her ski jacket. "Lauren thought you might need this until the car warms up," he said.

Kelly took the nylon-shelled jacket and zipped it over her arms. The bulky padding made her feel clumsy, but it was deliciously warm.

"Thanks," she said.

"Don't I take good care of you?" Marshall said. He escorted the girls out of the room and back across the slushy snow of the parking lot. Only Marshall knew their destination.

# TWELVE

The sky was gray in every direction. The road below was covered in a slush of half-melted snow. The wind whistled past the Mustang, pushing the car sideways and blowing streamers of snow through the sagebrush at the side of the highway.

Lauren had the heat on high, but very little made it to the backseat. Kelly huddled with her knees drawn up to her chest. It helped to keep her legs warm, but it did nothing for her freezing feet.

Lauren leaned over the steering wheel, staring intently at the treacherous road. Beside her Marshall slumped in his seat and nursed a soda Lauren had purchased when they stopped for gas that morning. He wouldn't let Lauren play the radio, not even for weather bulletins. It was obvious that he still hadn't worked off his hangover.

It had started to snow again soon after they had gotten on the road. At first it had been only scattered flakes, but by noon it was a steady fall, almost a blizzard. The flakes came in sheets, looking gray in the Mustang's headlights. Lauren had to keep the wipers on high just to keep the windows clear. And from the look of the overcast sky, it wasn't going to stop any time soon.

The traffic was thinner than it had been the evening before. Apparently many people had decided to sit out the storm where they were. The farther they went, the smarter that idea seemed. They passed several accidents—tractor trailers overturned in the median of the highway, cars almost buried in the drifts along the road, vehicles of all sorts that had smacked into each other or the railing.

Lauren asked to stop several times. The Mustang handled well in dry weather, but it was out of its element in the snow. The wide rear tires slipped constantly, and Lauren wrenched at the wheel to keep them in their lane.

"Please," she said after fighting the car through a drift that had started to grow out on the interstate. "It's getting worse. Can't we stop now?"

"Keep going," Marshall said.

"But I'm getting tired."

"Then Kelly can drive for a while."

"I'm not very good at driving in the snow," Kelly said.

"I guess you'd better hope it clears up soon," Marshall said. Then he slumped back in his seat. But the weather didn't improve. It got worse.

By two in the afternoon it was as dark as midnight, and the snow was falling so fast, the wipers couldn't handle it at any speed. The snowdrifts on the side of the road quickly spread across the highway, and soon the Mustang was up to its floorboards in snow. The car jumped and slipped. The snow underneath groaned as they plowed through.

If there were any other vehicles still traveling through the gloom, they were invisible behind the wall of snow. Kelly suspected that the only way they'd ever know if another car was near would be if they ran into it.

A green sign was visible for a moment through a gap in the snowstorm. "There's an exit just ahead," Kelly called, yelling to be heard over the howling wind and groaning snow. "We better take it."

"No," Marshall said. "We keep going."

The car bumped as they passed over a drift, and for a moment the engine raced as the wheels lost traction. "We can't keep going," Lauren protested. "We're going to get trapped soon."

"Keep going," Marshall said.

153

"Look," Kelly yelled, "you might be able to shoot us, but it won't keep you from freezing to death if the car gets stuck in this storm. We need to find a place to wait it out. Then we can go as far as you want."

"All right, pull over," he said. "But we go on as soon as it clears."

Lauren had a hard time getting up the exit ramp. It was covered in snow at least six inches deep, and the Mustang's tail swung back and forth like a pendulum as the tires sought some grip on the gentle slope. Kelly was afraid that someone would have to get out and push—and she knew that someone would not be Marshall—but Lauren worked the gas skillfully, and the car crested the exit ramp with enough momentum to slide out into the street.

The dark form of a motel was visible ahead. They couldn't see it all, but it was obviously a big place. Lauren missed the entrance to the parking lot and drove across the low median, smashing several small bushes on the way to the front office.

"Kelly," Marshall said. "You get the room this time."

"All right."

"And remember, pay cash. Do you have enough money?"

"I think so."

"Then get in there and be quick about it."

The wind was so strong that it almost knocked Kelly down when she stepped out of the car. Her legs sank to the knee in the fresh-fallen snow, and her already chilly feet became instantly numb. She struggled to the door of the motel, kicked off as much snow as she could, and stepped inside.

The motel was not only big, it was new and much fancier than the places where they had been staying. The lobby featured a huge fireplace that put out a welcome warmth, and long leather couches flanked by tall potted plants. The entrance to a restaurant was visible at the rear of the lobby. Signs pointed to a lounge, a health club, and an indoor pool.

The pool reminded Kelly that her swimsuit was packed in her suitcase. She had brought it along because the ski resort where they had been heading had hot tubs. Now the swimsuit was just as useless as her skis.

She walked across the tiled floor to the reception desk. Behind the desk was a young man with sandy hair and warm brown eyes.

"Good afternoon," he said pleasantly. "Checking in?"

"Yes," Kelly said. "I need a room for myself, and my . . . cousins. Three people, all together."

"Do you have a reservation?"

155

"No." She waved a hand toward the door. "The storm made us stop."

"I see." He sorted through some cards on his desk. "Well, we're really supposed to be full tonight, but half those people are probably stuck somewhere else. If you promise not to tell my boss, I'll forge a reservation for you."

"Thanks."

"What's your name?"

"Kelly Tallon."

He pulled a card out of a drawer and wrote down her name. "And your address?" As she gave it to him, he started shaking his head. "That's a shame," he said.

"What?"

"It's a shame that you live so far away," he said. He looked up at her and smiled. It was a quirky, off-center smile, but it was so obviously nice, so real, that Kelly wondered how she had ever been taken in by Marshall's imitation.

"Well, Kelly Tallon," he said. "Here's a card that says you called in a reservation two weeks ago, and here's the key to your room."

"Thanks again," she said. "I really appreciate it." She reached for the key and felt his fingers grip hers gently.

"If you want to show me how much you appreciate it," he said, "why not have dinner with

156

me tonight? The restaurant here's not very intimate, but the food is good."

After everything she'd been through, Kelly was surprised to find that she could still blush. "I don't think I can," she said.

"If you change your mind, you'll know where to find me. My name's Bill, and I'll be out here until six."

"Okay, Bill." Kelly took the key and went back across the lobby. She paused at the door. It was hard to face the idea of going back out into the snow, where Marshall waited with his gun. It would be much easier to run back over to Bill and tell him everything that had happened. But Lauren was out there, and if Kelly believed one thing that Marshall had said, it was that he wouldn't hesitate to kill her.

Marshall didn't seem concerned with how long it had taken Kelly to get the room. He even agreed to let Kelly carry in her suitcase. She fell twice as she slogged across the snowbound parking lot. He didn't help her up.

Their room turned out to be on the first floor near the front of the motel. It was really two rooms: a suite with two phones and a huge bathroom whose tub could have held four people at once.

"Wow," Lauren said. "How much did this place cost?"

"I don't know," Kelly replied, looking around the room in wonder. "I didn't pay yet."

Marshall's fingers closed on her shoulder like a vise. "You didn't pay?"

Kelly tried to pull away. "Not yet. You have to pay when you leave."

Marshall shoved her, and she stumbled across the room. Her heavy suitcase thudded on the carpeted floor. "Next time follow instructions." He strolled across the room, running his fingers over a gleaming marble countertop. "I like this place."

Kelly bent to pick up her suitcase.

Lauren switched on the television, and the dramatic music of a soap opera filled the room. "We haven't even watched TV in days," she said. "It feels like we've been in some other country."

*We have*, thought Kelly.

The beds were wide, with ornate brass headboards. Instead of tying their hands behind their backs, Marshall put them on separate beds and lashed their wrists to the headboards.

"Where are you going to sleep?" Lauren asked.

"Don't worry about me, sweetheart," Marshall said. "When I get back, we'll have some fun." He went over to Kelly's suitcase and flipped open the latches. "Let's see what we can find. You got those socks out of your mouths last night, so we'll have to find something better."

He pawed through Kelly's clothes, tossing them carelessly aside. Kelly had been looking forward to the chance to wear something clean, but now that Marshall had handled them, none of her clothes would seem clean. He stopped when he found a pair of knee socks. But this time, instead of pushing them into their mouths, he pulled them tight across their lips and tied the stretched socks at the back of their heads.

"Let's see you get that off," Marshall said. He paused by the mirror to give his hair a final inspection, then stepped out of the room.

Kelly tried to open her mouth, but the sock only peeled her lips back farther. At least when they were tied up this way, they were able to move their feet and look around. But they couldn't work together to get free. She turned her head to look at Lauren.

Lauren had pulled herself up the bed until she was sitting with her bound arms almost straight out at the side. Her gaze was fixed on the television screen, where beautiful actors spoke lines someone else had written and looked at each other with sparkling eyes.

For Kelly the soap opera didn't seem like something from another country; it seemed like something from another world. She couldn't imagine how Lauren could watch it. But tied up like they were, there was nothing else to do. She watched for a few minutes, letting the images pass without trying to understand them. Then she heard a soft noise from Lauren's bed.

It took Kelly a minute to figure out what Lauren was doing. She was leaning against the bed frame, swaying back and forth and moving her hands up and down as if she was listening to some music that Kelly couldn't hear. Kelly saw how frayed the leather laces had become, and realized what Lauren was up to: She was sawing through her bonds by rubbing them on the bedposts.

Kelly felt the back of the bed frame on her own bed. The front of the headboard was slick and polished, but it was unfinished and rough behind. Kelly began to imitate Lauren, scuffing the laces against the rough edge of metal. It wasn't long before she saw strands of leather peeling away.

There was a pop, and Kelly looked up to see one of Lauren's hands free. She reached up and pulled the sock over her head. "We're going to make it this time," Lauren said. "This time he was too smart for his own good." She tugged at the lace on her other wrist.

There was a knock at the door. Both girls froze, their eyes locked on the door.

"It's Marshall," Lauren whispered.

160

Kelly shook her head. Marshall wouldn't knock.

"Kelly?" called a voice at the door. "It's Bill."

Lauren frowned and looked at Kelly. "Who's Bill?"

Kelly nodded enthusiastically.

"Wait a second." Lauren leaned across the gap between the beds, stretching to her limits to snare the sock around Kelly's head and pull it free. "Now let's try it again. Who is Bill?"

Kelly didn't bother to reply. Instead she yelled toward the door. "Bill! We're in here! Help!"

Lauren followed Kelly's lead and started to yell herself. There was a rattling at the door, and a moment latter it sprang open. Bill flew into the room with a huge key chain held up like a club. He stumbled to a stop when he saw the two girls tied to the bed.

"What's going on here?" he asked.

"Get us loose!" Lauren cried.

"We've been kidnapped," Kelly said. "Get us out of here before the kidnapper comes back."

"Kidnapped?" Bill said. He looked around the room as if he expected someone to jump out from the corner.

"Hurry," Kelly urged. "We've got to get out of here before he comes back."

"He's a killer!" Lauren shouted.

Lauren's words made Bill's eyes widen, but he didn't run away. Instead he dropped to his knees beside Kelly's bed and fumbled at the laces. "Where's your other cousin?" he asked as he worked.

"Other cousin?"

"Didn't you check in with two cousins?"

"Oh," Kelly said. "The other one is the kidnapper."

Bill stopped and looked up at her with a puzzled expression. "You were kidnapped by your cousin?"

"No, no. He's not my cousin. He . . . oh, just hurry and get us out of here before he comes back."

It took only a minute to get Kelly loose. Then Bill turned his attention to Lauren's one remaining bond. In a few more seconds they were ready to go.

"Do you need anything out of here?" Bill asked.

"I don't think so," Kelly said. "If we do, we can get it after the police come."

Bill paused at the door on the way out and looked at Kelly with his crooked grin. "And to think, I just came to see if you'd changed your mind about dinner."

"Bill," Kelly said. "I'll be happy to have dinner with you."

He laughed.

The door flew open, spinning Bill around and driving him back into the room. He staggered back another step, as Kelly and Lauren stood paralyzed behind him.

For Kelly everything was happening in slow motion. She saw Marshall step into the room. She saw the gun in his hand and the gleam of his smile as he raised the barrel. The light in his blue eyes was like a neon sign.

Then the gun went off, and time snapped back to normal. Bill fell to the side, glancing off the wall. Marshall fired again, and Bill doubled over backward with his knees under him. His eyes stared sightlessly up at the ceiling. His mouth was open in an O of surprise.

"Sorry to spoil your dinner plans, Bill," Marshall said. "But that's the way it goes."

# THIRTEEN

Kelly leaned over Bill and reached out a hand to his face. A single drop of blood ran down his cheek like a scarlet tear. At Kelly's touch he slumped to the side and crumpled to the floor.

Vaguely she could hear people shouting, doors slamming, feet running. Lauren was screaming. But all of that seemed far away. She felt sleepy. It seemed like the best idea in the world to just lie down here on the carpet and sleep for days and days.

A hand jerked her up from the floor. "Move now," Marshall said. "Or I'll kill you."

Kelly wasn't sure that sounded so bad, but she let Marshall push her out of the motel room and down the hallway. A woman in a robe and shower cap opened a door ahead of them, took one look, and then slammed the door again. Kelly found that terribly funny, and laughed all the rest of the way down the hall.

Marshall opened the door to the parking lot, and Kelly was suddenly aware that her coat and all the rest of her luggage was back in the motel room. That was funny too. Wind whipped her hair around her face. It was still snowing, and the cars outside were little more than white lumps in the snow. Fat flakes of snow blew over the cars, and there weren't even any tracks in the parking lot. Kelly thought that was hilarious.

"Be quiet," Marshall said.

That was the funniest thing of all, and Kelly laughed even harder.

"Shut up," Marshall said. He slapped her. Hard.

Kelly wanted to keep laughing, but she couldn't remember why everything had seemed so funny. She wanted to, because funny was something she could definitely use, but it was gone. She was standing in the snow-blanketed parking lot, shivering in her sweater.

"We can't go anywhere in this," Lauren said.

"Get in the car and drive," Marshall said.

"Look at it!" Lauren shouted. She waved a hand at the snow. "Even if we get out of the parking lot, we can't go anywhere."

166

Marshall fired a shot that missed Lauren by inches and crashed through the windshield of a car behind her. "Get in the car," he said.

Marshall shoved Kelly into the backseat and took his spot in the front. Lauren worked wonders in getting the Mustang out of its parking slot and nursing it onto the highway. By the time they went sliding away, quite a crowd had gathered at the door of the motel. Their faces looked red in the glow of the Mustang's taillights. Several of them were pointing toward the car. Kelly didn't mention that to Marshall.

There was no way to tell where the exit from the parking lot was. And the road beyond was a guess. The car bounced over buried obstacles, and Kelly struck her head against the roof. They went down the ramp to the interstate in one prolonged slide, but once they were back on the interstate, it wasn't as bad as Kelly had expected.

Snowplows had gone past while they were in the motel, and the new snow hadn't quite matched the previous depth. They bumped along with no sound but the grinding of the snow under the tires and the hiss of the flakes whipping past the car.

They hadn't been on the road ten minutes before Kelly was wondering if they had ever really stopped at a motel. She remembered checking in, and the brass beds, and Bill getting shot. But it all seemed so distant, like the soap-opera images she had glimpsed on the motel TV.

Blue lights came out of the gloom. As they drew closer, the form of three black-and-white police cars could be seen.

"Just keep driving," Marshall said. He watched the police cars go past on the other side of the interstate. "We've got to get off this road."

Kelly looked along the side of the highway. In some places the drifts were higher than the car, and the dirty snow thrown up by the plows made a formidable barrier. "You're sure you want to get off?" she asked.

"At the next exit," Marshall said. "We'll get off there."

The next exit was a long time in coming. Another police car went by in the opposite lane, followed by an ambulance with its red light flashing.

*That ambulance is for Bill*, Kelly thought. But it still didn't seem real. Marshall had killed Bill. There was no impact, none at all.

It was very cold in the backseat. The vinyl was stiff and the few gusts of heat that made it back to Kelly only reminded her of how cold she was.

An exit finally came up. There was nothing at this one, not even a gas station. According to the signs, there was a highway that ran across the interstate, but beyond the obvious trail of the overpass railings, it was impossible to pick the road out of the flat expanse of snow.

"What now?" Lauren asked.

"Turn south."

"Which way?"

"Left. Turn left."

There were no tracks to follow, and the Mustang plowed a wake as it rode down the slope away from the interstate. Without the plows and the traffic, the snow here had not been compacted. In many places that was good, because the wind had scoured the road clean. But in other places drifts the size of small houses edged the road and trailed waist-deep tails across the blacktop.

Headlights appeared behind them. Marshall stared back between the seats, looking at the lights through the rear window. "Funny, nobody on this road for hours, then somebody turns off right behind us." He turned to Lauren. "Drive faster."

"If I drive any faster, we'll have a wreck."

"Drive faster," he repeated.

Kelly watched the headlights behind them as they bounced and weaved around the drifts. The police are after us because Marshall killed Bill. This time the memory brought with it images of Bill's brown eyes and crooked grin. And it brought pain. Kelly was glad to feel even pain.

"The police are going to catch you," she said.

"You better hope not," Marshall said. "Because if they catch me, they catch you, too."

"We haven't done anything," Lauren said.

"Haven't done anything?" he said. "Haven't you sheltered a known criminal for days and driven him halfway across the country?"

"You forced us to do that," Kelly said.

"You want to ask the people at all the places we've stopped if you were forced?" Marshall snorted. "Why, the way I remember it, Lauren here was tired of being pushed around by her rich daddy and decided she wanted to play things a little fast and loose."

"They'll never believe that," Lauren said.

"I wouldn't be too sure, little girl. You spent two days telling me everything about yourself." He put on his best, most innocent smile. "I can be very convincing."

*He killed Bill. He killed the gas station attendant. He killed the man in the pickup truck. And there's no doubt, none at all, that he's going to kill us both.* Pain flooded in and brought with it a load of anger and fear. And this time Kelly didn't try to repress it.

She lunged out of her seat toward Marshall. He turned quickly and swung at her, but his arm glanced off the back of his car seat and the blow missed. She wasn't sure what she meant to do until she did it. What she did was reach past Marshall, grab the door handle, and push open the passenger door.

Lauren slammed on the brakes, but instead of skidding to a stop, the Mustang went into a spin.

Kelly was hurled from one side of the car to the other. She saw that Marshall had his gun in one hand and his satchel in the other. That left him with no hands to hold on. She screamed, and jumped at him.

The gun went off, and she felt the bullet passing close by her ear. The car seemed to be spinning faster, the headlights giving glimpses of road, drifts, snow-covered fields. Kelly was almost in the front seat with Marshall, and she was kicking, punching, doing everything to push him toward the open door.

She saw him leaning into the void, whirling the hand with the satchel like an acrobat trying to balance on a high wire.

Kelly screamed. She didn't scream any words; it was the scream itself that felt good. She put her feet on him and kicked. She punched with her hands. And she kept screaming.

Despite the pressure she put on him, Marshall managed to hook his elbows on the door frame and regain his balance. He started to shove himself back into his seat. The gun barrel came up again, and his lips moved in some threat, but Kelly couldn't hear it over the wind.

Lauren let go of the wheel and swung at him. Her hand missed Kelly by a fraction of an inch and hit Marshall just above the eye, and he slipped back several inches. She swung again, and her fist struck his straight nose.

There was a new look on Marshall's face, a mixture of surprise and fear.

Kelly kicked at his legs, and his feet went skidding over the wet floormat. He was almost completely out the door now, and the force of the spinning car pulled at him.

At the last second Marshall dropped his gun and grabbed at the car seat. Kelly stomped on his hand as hard as she could.

Marshall fell out the open door.

As the car spun, the headlights swept over him like a strobe. In one sweep of the lights Kelly saw him strike the pavement. In the next he was tumbling along the road, his arms and legs bent at impossible angles. One more flash and he seemed to be still—a dark shape fading in the distance. Then the Mustang slammed into a snowdrift.

The car rolled onto its side. Kelly almost fell out the door herself, and she saw snow-covered blacktop sliding by beneath her dangling feet before the car rolled again. Now it was skating along on its roof. Kelly heard Lauren's home-made ski rack crack loose and grind between the car and the road. The Mustang rolled almost to the other side, then settled back on its roof.

Kelly had time to look over and see Lauren dangling from the wheel. Her hands were still trying to steer, even though none of the wheels was on the ground. Then the Mustang struck a more substantial drift. Kelly fell forward, her head striking the windshield only inches from the place where Marshall's forehead had starred the glass. The car made one last roll, landing on its side with the open passenger door facing down.

The car stopped moving. The engine coughed and died. The snow continued to come down, and in only a few minutes the hole they had made in the snowbank healed.

Inside the Mustang everything was very, very quiet.

# FOURTEEN

Kelly pushed at the door over her head. The hinges groaned, but it didn't open. She shifted her feet, hooking one foot on the steering wheel and planting the other on the parking brake, and tried again. This time the door opened with a grinding squeak. Snow and sunlight spilled down into the car. Kelly climbed onto the side of the driver's seat and stuck her head up into the day.

"Do you see anything?" Lauren called from where she sat at the bottom of the wreck.

"Yeah," Kelly said. "I see something."

"What?"

Kelly shook her head. "You aren't going to believe it."

The view outside was like nothing Kelly had

ever seen before. It wasn't the snow that covered everything in a gentle, undulating sheet—it was what she saw rising above the snow that shocked her. All around them great towers of jagged rock jutted hundreds of feet into the sky. Some stood alone and looked as sharp as knives; others were clumped together to form pale rock castles. The gray sides of the towers were stained with splashes of green and yellow and red.

Kelly eased herself back into the car and climbed down beside Lauren. "It looks like we've crashed on the moon," she said.

"Did you see any houses or other cars?" Lauren asked.

"Nothing. I didn't see anything but rock and snow."

"What about . . ." She hesitated and looked up at the open door. "What about Marshall?"

"No," Kelly said. "He must be buried under the snow."

Lauren closed her eyes and nodded. She put her right arm under her and tried to sit up. Kelly reached to help her. Lauren's other arm dangled limp at her side, broken in the crash.

"How does your side feel?" Kelly asked.

"Not too good. How about your head?"

Kelly touched the tender bump on her skull. A shock of pain that left her dizzy went through her. "It's better, I think. Listen, we're going to have to get out of here."

"And go where?"

"I don't know, but we can't wait here. There's not a single track in the snow out there. We're probably miles from where the police think we are. There might be nobody down this road for a week, and we'll freeze to death by then."

"I'm not sure I can get up," Lauren said.

"You have to," Kelly told her, "because I'm not leaving you here."

It took twenty terrible minutes to get Lauren out of the car. Her arm wasn't just broken—it was broken so badly that the jagged end of the bone pressed against her skin. And Kelly suspected that Lauren had broken several ribs as well. Her side was puffy, and the skin was slick and bruised. Kelly helped her climb down from the top of the wrecked car and into the soft drift.

"Wow," Lauren said as she looked around. "You weren't kidding. This is one weird place."

Once they were outside and away from the car, Kelly remembered just how cold it was. It had stopped snowing, but the sky showed only thin patches of blue and the air held the threat of more snow. The wind roared in from the north, cutting through their thin clothing.

"I'm going back into the car," Kelly told Lauren. "I'm going to get more of your clothes out of your suitcase. We'll need everything we have to keep warm."

Kelly burrowed into the car and dragged Lauren's suitcase from the back. She managed to get it to the top of the car and pitch it off into the snow. Then she climbed down and snapped it open. There was a jacket inside. She saved that for Lauren. For herself she pulled out two of Lauren's soft, expensive sweaters and slid them over the sweater she was already wearing.

Lauren was sitting in the snow, staring toward the open car door that jutted into the air. "Look at my Mustang," she said. "It's not even a year old. Just look at it."

Kelly did look, but except for the door and the few feet of the side they had exposed in climbing out, there was nothing to see but a lump in the snow. "Think of it this way," she said. "At least now you don't have to worry about the hail damage."

Lauren did not laugh.

Kelly got Lauren on her feet and helped her into the jacket. Lauren's face shone with sweat, and her lips were very pale. Kelly was beginning to suspect that Lauren might have not only broken ribs but some kind of internal injury.

"Come on," Kelly said gently. "Let's get moving."

"Which way?" Lauren asked.

Kelly opened her mouth to answer, then shut it again. It wasn't as easy a question as she'd thought.

The car had spun around so many times, there was no way to know if it was facing the way they had been traveling or back the way they'd come. Any tracks they had made had been erased by the wind. And the level stretch of snow that showed the location of the road looked the same in both directions.

"That way," Kelly said at last. She pointed down the road.

"Toward the biggest rocks?" Lauren asked.

Kelly nodded. "I think we'd have seen those things even in the dark. It's probably twenty miles back to the motel, and I don't remember a store, or even a house, between here and there. Let's take our chances going forward."

Walking through the snow was hard work. With every step Kelly sank past her knees. And though the layers of Lauren's sweaters were enough to keep her arms and chest warm, her feet were protected only by thin sneakers. They were numb before she had walked a hundred yards.

Kelly was suffering, but she knew it was

179

worse for Lauren. She held her broken arm tight across her side, but with every step, Kelly saw her wince in pain. Her normally tan skin looked very pasty.

The spires of rock never seemed to get any closer, but after only a few minutes of walking, Kelly looked back to see that the Mustang had been lost in the whiteness. Even their footsteps were being erased by the wind.

Lauren slipped and fell facedown in the snow. Kelly helped her up. A few minutes later she fell again. This time she didn't try to get up.

"Can we stop and rest?" she asked.

"I don't know," Kelly said. "I don't think it's such a good idea."

"Just a few minutes. I'm really feeling bad."

Kelly didn't like the idea of sitting in the snow—hypothermia was just around the corner even without giving it a hand—but one look at her friend's face was all it took to see just how serious things were getting. Lauren's lips weren't just pale—they were as white as the snow. And as cold as it was, fine beads of sweat ran down her forehead.

Kelly put a hand to her cheek. "Lauren! You're burning up."

"I know," she said. "World's fastest flu."

"It can't be the flu. I think you hurt yourself in the accident."

"I know I hurt myself in the wreck. Just look at my arm."

"It's not your arm I'm worried about," Kelly said. "It's that bruise on your side. I'm afraid you're bruised, or even bleeding, on the inside."

Lauren didn't seem too shocked by the idea. She just nodded her head. "I think you're right. I feel . . . funny. Like something in me is twisting when we walk. It doesn't hurt, but it feels really strange." She looked up at Kelly. "So what do we do about it?"

"We keep walking," Kelly said. "There's nothing else we can do." She helped Lauren up, and they struggled on down the road.

The rock towers finally seemed to be drawing nearer. Kelly could see crowns of snow clinging at the tops and ruffles of snow on ledges along the side. On a few of the ridges and crests, little clumps of dull-brown sage were visible. As pitiful as they were, Kelly was glad to see any sign of life.

Then Kelly fell in the snow. Her foot caught on some hidden obstacle, and she tumbled over, windmilling her arms and falling facedown in a drift. It took her a few seconds to realize that what had caught her foot was the top strand of a barbed-wire fence and a few seconds more to realize that they didn't put fences in the middle of the road.

181

"Are you okay?" Lauren asked.

"Yeah," Kelly replied, "but I'm not sure we're okay. We've gotten off the road." She looked at the flat plain around them. The snow formed gentle dunes, subtle hills with pale-blue shadows. But nothing gave a hint of where the road might run.

"Does it matter?"

"It does if we want to get somewhere. We'll have to go back until we find it."

Wearily Lauren turned and began to go back the way they'd come. Kelly followed her, stepping in her footprints and looking for anything that might mark the edge of the buried road.

Fortunately they had to backtrack only for a couple of minutes before Kelly saw what had happened. The road hadn't ended; it had intersected another highway in a T intersection.

"Another decision to make," she said. "Which way now?"

"Right," Lauren said immediately.

"Why?"

"Because I think you were right last time—we didn't come this way last night. And if I remember the turns we took last night, then right would be north. Back toward the interstate."

Kelly could barely remember any of the turns they'd taken during that wild ride. She hoped Lauren was remembering the course as well as she seemed to and not just imagining it out of her fever. The sun stubbornly hid behind the clouds, refusing to help indicate whether Lauren was correct about the direction.

"Right it is," Kelly said.

They trudged up the highway to the right, past the top two inches of a red stop sign sticking out of a drift, and on across the featureless plain. A few minutes later the ground began to slope upward, and the road curved back toward the towers of rock. Kelly was afraid they might lose the highway again if it didn't stay straight, but the snow wasn't as deep on the slope. The tops of rusty fences peeked out of the snow on both sides, conveniently bracketing the location of the road.

They were almost to the first of the stone pillars when Lauren found the sign. It was a wide green highway marker with an arrow pointing up the road in the direction they were traveling.

Kelly knelt to brush the snow away.

"What's it say?" Lauren asked.

"'Wall ten,'" Kelly said.

"What's Wall?"

Kelly shrugged. "A town maybe? And it must be ten miles away."

"Ten miles doesn't seem so bad," Lauren said. "I've walked farther than that before. We hiked almost sixteen miles when we were camping in Washington Park. Remember?"

"Right. We can do ten miles! Let's get moving."

Lauren turned and headed up the road, moving a little faster than before. She had sounded better when she talked about the ten-mile distance. Almost cheerful.

Kelly had tried to sound cheerful too. They had hiked sixteen miles back home, but it had been in the summer. They hadn't been freezing. Or starving. And neither of them had been suffering from broken bones and who-knew-what kind of internal injuries.

The wind picked up again, blowing Kelly's hair around her face so violently that it stung. *We didn't have to face a wind like this in Washington Park*, she thought. *Or wade chest-deep in snow.*

She looked up at the sky and saw that there were several more patches of blue than there had been when they started walking. But those patches were getting darker. Kelly knew there was no way they could make it into the town of Wall before nightfall. If this nightmare place wasn't bad enough, they'd soon be walking through it in the dark.

*At least it isn't snowing.*

But the first flakes fell even before Kelly could finish the thought.

# FIFTEEN

The snow came down, but it never seemed to hit the ground. The wind blew it so hard that it traveled along horizontally, stinging Kelly on her bare face and neck. It felt like needles against her cheeks. She hunched her shoulders and lowered her chin, but it wasn't much help.

The road sloped up, and the cliffs to the left and right of the road grew higher and steeper the farther they walked. The towers of stone pointed to the gray sky. The silence of the place was eerie. There were no car horns—no cars. Nothing but the passing wind and the hissing snow.

"How far?" Lauren said.

Kelly turned to her, squinting against the snow. "How far to what?"

"How far have we gone? Since we saw the sign, I mean."

"I think about a mile."

"Is that all?"

"Maybe more like two," Kelly said, but it was a lie. Lauren had started out with renewed energy after they'd seen the sign. For a short while she seemed almost well. But she wasn't well; she was very ill. And after a few minutes her pace had slowed to a crawl. Far from believing they'd gone two miles, Kelly doubted that they'd gone even one.

Kelly wasn't feeling too well herself. Her head pounded from its collision with the Mustang's windshield, and another dozen bruises she had picked up in the crash were starting to make themselves known. And she was cold: her head was cold, her hands were icy, and her feet had been numb so long, she worried that she had frostbite up to her knees. She stopped for a moment to fight off a bout of dizziness and nausea.

When she looked up again, she decided that she'd have to add optical illusions to her growing lists of problems. Stretching across this narrow winding road, in the middle of this desolate wilderness, were what looked like tollbooths.

"Kelly, what is that?" Lauren said.

"You see it too?"

"Of course. It looks like the booths on the highway."

"I know," Kelly said. "But it can't be. Come on, let's see what it really is."

They didn't have to go as far as she'd thought. The answer actually came a hundred yards before they reached the strange booths. Another sign stuck up out of the snow at the edge of the road. When Kelly brushed it clean with her frozen fingers, it showed words written in white on brown.

WELCOME TO
BADLANDS
NATIONAL PARK

"A national park?" Lauren said numbly as if she'd never heard of such a thing.

"Yep," Kelly said. *Badlands*, she thought. *We've been going through badlands ever since we left home.* Despite the name, the sign brought Kelly a feeling of hope, the first she'd felt in hours. It swept over her and warmed her.

"They made a national park out of this place?"

"All these rocks and cliffs are kind of spectacular. It's probably prettier and a lot easier to get around in the summer. Besides, a national park means park rangers." Kelly couldn't keep the smile off her face. "Rangers that are probably right up there at the entrance. Come on!"

Kelly charged into the snow like someone running through ocean waves. Lauren ran at her side, and though her breath hissed between her teeth as she fought back the pain of her arm and side, she didn't stumble or slow until they reached the entrance gate.

The two buildings guarding the entrance to the park were larger than tollbooths, but just barely. The one on the left was obviously closed—its smoked-glass windows were dark, and a barrier projected from its side to block the snow-choked road. But the other booth glowed with lights, and the door on its side gaped open.

"Hello!" Kelly called. "Can you help us?" She climbed over the compacted snow around the booth and stepped down into the almost-clear area by the door. "Hello?" she called again.

She pushed at the door, and it opened easily. There was a green plastic lawn chair in the center of the booth. A shelf in the back had stacks of brown leaflets that carried the name of the park in bright letters. Beside them was a white plastic case whose front carried a large red cross. A black telephone clung to the wall.

Lauren slid down the snow to stand beside Kelly. "Where's the ranger?" she asked.

"Not home," Kelly told her, "but he left us a phone."

It was an odd telephone. It didn't have a dial or buttons, but as soon as Kelly picked it up, it started to ring. It rang three times. Four. "Come on, come on," Kelly said softly. "Somebody answer." The phone continued to ring.

"What's wrong?" Lauren asked.

"Nobody's picking up." Kelly gave up after twenty rings. "It's just not my week for telephones. I wonder where it was ringing, anyway."

"Probably up there." Lauren wiped snow away from her eyes and pointed past the booths.

Kelly turned and saw a group of buildings through the driving snow. A small house was flanked by several gray metal buildings that could have been storage sheds, and the dark, round shape of a satellite dish. They were all huddled together on a small flat area at the edge of a cliff.

The snow between the entrance booths and the house had been shoveled recently to make an almost-clear path. Fresh snow had started to fill in the path, but patches of blacktop still showed through.

"That must be where the rangers live," Kelly said.

"Great. Then let's get over there."

"Wait a second." Kelly ducked into the

189

booth and grabbed the white first-aid kit. She opened it and dug through the contents. There were bandages and ointments, some of which would probably help with Lauren's arm, but Kelly didn't know enough about first aid to use them properly. There was a bottle of aspirin, and that was something she could use. The child-protector top was almost too much for her stiff, cold fingers, but eventually she got it open.

"Here," she said, handing a pair of the white tablets to Lauren. "This might help the pain, and it'll get your fever down."

Lauren took the pills from her and choked them down. "Can we go now?"

Kelly looked around. It was starting to get dark, and the colors of the rock spires had faded to shades of gray. Even the snow reflected the slatelike color of the darkening sky. Against this frozen, forbidding background, the little house was a beacon of warmth. Yellow light spilled out from curtained windows, and a bright-green welcome mat was visible through a dusting of snow on the porch.

"Yeah, let's go," she said. "Even if there's nobody home, we'll be okay."

"You sure?"

"Absolutely. We'll be warm, and we'll have food, and there's bound to be a real phone over there."

Lauren leaned against the entrance booth with her good arm. "I just want to go home."

"Then let's go home," Kelly said.

Lauren pushed herself away from the booth and started shuffling up the path. Kelly followed close behind.

Kelly was no wilderness scout, but from the many footprints, it was obvious that more than one person had gone up the path since the snow had started falling again. They climbed up onto the front step, and Lauren rapped on the door. "I hear someone," she said.

Kelly heard voices too, but they had the distinctive tinniness of a radio or television show. "Knock again."

Lauren pounded the door harder, and it creaked open. Light and the sound of canned laughter spilled out. "I don't like this," Lauren said.

"I'm sure it's okay," Kelly said. "The ranger is probably out . . . rangering." She stepped past Lauren into the house.

"Hello," she called. "Anyone home?" The front room was tiny. There was no furniture except a stained coffee table with a lamp and a threadbare recliner. The worn carpet was almost covered in knee-high stacks of books. As shabby as it was, the room was deliciously warm.

"Park rangers have to live in this place?"

Lauren said from the doorway. "Out here by themselves?"

"They're dedicated," Kelly said.

She walked around the stacks and through the doorway into the kitchen. The refrigerator was new, but the other appliances were old and dented. There was no dining table. Instead, a counter ran most of the way across the room. A neat stack of dishes rested on the counter. Beside the dishes a pile of silverware lay wrapped in a yellow towel.

There was a smell of hot metal in the air. Kelly stepped forward, sniffing.

There was a pan on the stove. The pan was empty, but the burner under it glowed cherry-red. Kelly took another half step toward the stove, reaching out to turn off the burner. Then she saw the boots.

The boots were scuffed brown leather with heavy rubber soles and long leather laces like the ones Marshall had used to tie Kelly and Lauren. Drops of water that must have come from melted snow still clung to the sides of the boots. They were sticking out from behind the breakfast counter.

With her hand still frozen in the air from reaching toward the stove, Kelly stepped around the counter. There were pants legs that ran into the boots. And a shirt above the pants. There

192

was a long moment in which that was all Kelly could see—the boots, the pants, and the shirt. It took longer to see the body.

The park ranger had been a small woman with dark-blond hair pulled back in a ponytail. Her arms were stretched out across the floor. A glass lay on the tile beside her in the middle of a pool of milk. Her pale gray eyes looked up at the ceiling from a face that was surprisingly calm.

Kelly stumbled back a step. "Lauren! We've got to get out of here."

"Oh, I think it's too late for that, sweetheart," Marshall said.

Kelly whirled around and saw him standing beside the doorway with his arm locked around Lauren's throat. There was no doubt that it was Marshall, but the attractive guy that Lauren had stopped to help was gone. In his place was a monster.

His face was as puffy as an old melon, and his blue eyes peered from dark pits in the swollen flesh. His skin was torn. Dried blood caked his cheeks. The hand that was clamped over Lauren's mouth was dark and twisted. His jeans and his jacket were tattered.

He smiled. Dark gaps of broken teeth marred his perfect smile. His lips were swollen and split. "You can't imagine how happy I am to see you two girls."

Kelly stepped back into the kitchen and slid past the hot stove. She stretched her hand back across the counter, feeling for the silverware. "Let her go."

Marshall stepped through the kitchen door, forcing Lauren ahead of him. "I don't think so," he said. "I don't think so."

Kelly's hand felt the outlines of a knife. It wasn't huge, but it was a knife. She wrapped her fingers around it, whipped it from behind her, and held it with the point angled toward Marshall's battered face.

"Let her go now!"

Marshall smiled again. Blood trickled from the corner of his mouth. "I can break her neck before you take a step."

"I'll kill you," Kelly said. She was amazed at how calm her voice sounded, even though her heart was pounding like a bass drum in her ears.

"You'll try," Marshall said. "I know you'll try. But this is the end of the line, little Kelly." He took a half step back into the tiny front room. "I'm going to have to kill you both now. Sorry about that."

As injured as he was, he still managed to sound sincere.

# SIXTEEN

Kelly didn't wait for Marshall to move first. She lunged toward him, slashing the air with her knife.

Marshall pivoted, putting Lauren between them like a shield. "Oh, a knife. You'd better be careful, little girl. You wouldn't want to scratch your friend," he said.

"Why not? You're going to kill her anyway." Kelly jumped again.

She missed, but this time Marshall released his grip on Lauren and shoved her away. Kelly stabbed at him again, and he caught her arm as it drove upward with the knife. He shoved her back against the stove and stepped in close. Slowly he began to turn her arm and force the knife back toward her.

Trembling as she fought to resist him, Kelly's fingers opened and she dropped the knife. It thudded on the kitchen floor. Still holding Kelly's arm, Marshall bent to pick up the knife. Kelly drove her knee into his swollen face.

Marshall grunted in surprise and pain. He released Kelly's arm and fell back. He lay on the floor for a second, and Kelly thought he might be unconscious, but then he jumped back onto his feet and swung at her.

Kelly didn't realize he was holding the knife until it sliced into the sweaters at her throat. It snagged in the many layers of cloth. She could feel the point against her skin. She was afraid to even breathe.

He pulled the knife free and grinned at her with the stumps of his bloody teeth. "Good-bye, Kelly," he said, then plunged the knife toward her chest.

There was a hollow thud, and the knife fell from his hand. Marshall staggered to the side, and Kelly saw Lauren standing behind him with a lamp in her good arm. "Are you okay?" she had time to say, and then Marshall was up again, shoving Lauren back into the front room.

Kelly jumped at him, pounding her fists into his back. He spun and caught her by the throat. He squeezed until his fingers cut off the air and blackness hovered at the edge of Kelly's vision.

He jerked his arm up until only the tips of her toes were still on the ground. Slowly he brought back his other hand and balled the fingers into a fist. His arm jabbed forward, and Marshall's fist struck Kelly on the chin.

This was no slap to get her attention; it was a crushing blow that sent her flying across the room. She smashed into the counter, and it collapsed onto the floor in a heap of wood and metal. She lay there in the wreckage of the counter while bells and sirens echoed in her skull. Distantly she heard yelling and fighting, and the front door banged shut twice.

Kelly wasn't sure how long she lay there. Eventually she climbed to her feet and stepped across the kitchen to the front room. The books that had been stacked so neatly were now scattered over the floor. The worn chair was overturned, and the table lay on its side beside the wall.

"Lauren?" Kelly called softly.

The front door opened again, and Marshall stepped back in.

"Where's Lauren? What have you done to her?"

"One down," he said, "and one to go."

He stepped into the room, and Kelly saw that his left leg was as stiff as deadwood. He advanced on her with his arms outstretched, blood running from fresh scratches on his face and his injured leg dragging behind him.

Kelly's mind suddenly flashed the image of the mummy in an old horror movie. In the midst of everything she almost laughed. She had been close to hysteria ever since she had first seen the gun in Marshall's hand back in Kansas, and now she was almost ready to give in to it.

She backed into the kitchen and pulled the empty pan from the still-glowing burner. "Stay back," she said as he took another dragging step. She swung the pan at his head.

He blocked her swing with his forearm, stopping the pan inches from his face. "There's no one to save you this time, Kelly," he said. Then he grabbed the side of the pan.

Marshall's fingers sizzled as they touched the hot metal. His blue eyes bulged in his damaged face. A whimper started down in his throat and grew into a noise that was not a scream or a shout, but simply a pure expression of pain.

He pulled his hand away, and the skin of his fingers was ashy white.

Kelly swung the pan at him again, and Marshall stumbled back. He looked at Kelly, then down at his smoking hand, then back at Kelly.

"Where's Lauren?" she shouted.

She swung a third time. He tried to duck

back, but the pan glanced off his cheek, causing him to cry out again. Marshall faced her for a moment longer, then turned and staggered out the front door with his injured leg dragging behind.

Trembling and holding the pan out in front of her, Kelly walked to the door. It was very dark, and snow streaked across the yellow rectangle of light that spilled out the door. There was a crumpled form draped across the edge of the step.

"Lauren!" Kelly dropped the pan and rushed outside.

Lauren was lying on her side. A frosting of snow covered her dark hair. When Kelly rolled her over, she saw that Lauren's eyes were rolled back to show only whites. Blood streamed from her nose. In the light from the house, the blood was amazingly bright. In the snow where Lauren lay, it made a startling pink stain.

"Oh, Lauren," Kelly whispered.

There was a blur of movement, and Kelly was thrown into the snow. She climbed to her knees, but before she could get to her feet, hands grabbed at her back and shoved her down again. Her hand searched for the ground in front of her and found only air. Dimly she realized that she was at the edge of the cliff on which the house was perched. She was shoved again and then flipped over to lie faceup in the snow.

Marshall stood over her, his breath puffing out in the cold air. "Now you're going to die," he hissed.

Kelly kicked his injured leg and he toppled into the snow. "You keep saying that," she screamed back at him. "But you're the one that's going to die." Before he could rise, she kicked him again and drew a satisfying gasp of pain.

She tried for a third kick, but Marshall's hand closed on her ankle and he flipped her away. Away and off the cliff.

Kelly found herself spinning through space. She brushed against hard stone. The cliff face was bare of snow, and her hands felt rocks and frozen earth sliding past. Then she was back in the air. She had time to wonder how far it was to the bottom. As the seconds passed, it seemed clear that it was more than far enough to kill her.

It was the snow that saved her.

The snow at the base of the cliff had drifted into a huge frozen wave that reared a dozen feet into the air. Kelly fell into it with a force that drove the air from her lungs and left her struggling for breath. But the cushioning of the snow kept her from being broken on the barren ground.

Kelly came up sputtering and gasping from

the snowdrift like a diver coming out of deep water. By the time she was able to draw a breath, she had tumbled to the base of the drift. She lay there gasping and staring up at the dark cliff face.

The line between the sky and the edge of the cliff was hard to make out, but Kelly thought she could see it high above her. For a moment she even imagined she could see someone moving around on the edge of the cliff, but she knew that had to be her imagination.

Looking up, she realized just how long the fall had been, and how lucky she had been to survive it. She felt a strange mixture of triumph and fear.

Then she remembered Lauren. Lauren was up there, either dead or dying, and there was no one with her but Marshall.

Kelly rolled out of the snowdrift and stood up. She wondered how long it would take her to climb the cliff. *Forever. That's how long*, she thought.

There was no way she could get back up the cliff. She tried to think back to what she had seen during the day. The ground had been almost level at the spot where the Mustang had crashed. It was only when they had started up the road that led to the park that the ground had begun to rise.

So if Kelly walked back along the cliff toward the Mustang, then the cliffs would be smaller. There was no way she could walk all the way back to the car—even if Lauren wasn't dead already, she'd be frozen by the time Kelly made such a long trip. And Kelly doubted she had the energy left to make the trip herself. She'd just have to follow the cliff back until she came to an easy place to climb. *There has to be a place like that*, she told herself. *Has to be*.

She had to get away from the cliff face to walk; the snowdrifts were too deep close to the wall. Away from the bluff, the wind had blown the snow into a series of dunes. The ground between the dunes was almost bare. Kelly walked through these bare patches, stepping over isolated sage bushes and chunks of ice-crusted rock.

Every hundred steps she pushed through the drifts to the side of the cliff, looking for a place to get back to the top. *If I can just get back to the top*, she thought, *everything will be okay*.

Suddenly Kelly realized that when she got back to the top, Marshall would be waiting for her.

*No, he won't. He's got to think he killed me. Even if he's still up there, I'll surprise him. I'll save Lauren, find a telephone, and go home.*

When she finally found a place where the

steep side of the cliff was sliced by a narrow gully, she didn't hesitate for a second but stepped right in and started climbing.

The gully was easy for the first few yards, but it quickly got steeper. Kelly had to get down on her hands and knees to push herself up. In the dark it was hard to find places to plant her hands and feet, and her frozen limbs made her clumsy. But none of that mattered to her now, because her tired mind was focused on going home.

She couldn't see the top of the cliff as she started to climb, but it soon became apparent to her that she had turned the wrong way in her confusion after the fall. She hadn't been walking back toward the car, but away from it. And all the time she had been walking, the cliff had been growing higher.

Kelly labored for what seemed like hours, and by the time she realized her mistake, she was at least a hundred feet above ground. Kelly knew that if she was ever going to go home, she would have to keep climbing, no matter how many hundreds of feet of wind-swept rock waited over her head. All of it would have to be climbed.

# SEVENTEEN

Kelly had never been cold before. She remembered playing in the snow when she was little, and her first ski trip when she hadn't known what to wear. Those had been times when she had thought she was cold. But those had been slight chills. They couldn't compare with the painful, lung-tightening coldness that held her now.

Kelly had never been tired before, either. She had never reached the point where every muscle in her body—from the tips of her skinned and bleeding fingers to the tips of her frozen and battered toes—twitched in uncontrollable spasms.

The climb had taken hours. Hours of being buffeted by winds and blasted by snow. Kelly knew it was hours and not days only because the sun had not come up. It was coming up now, coming up red and strong in a deep-blue sky.

Kelly stood on a ledge of icy stone that was barely as wide as her feet. Her left hand held a tiny nubbin of rock above her, while her right hand scrambled over the wall, trying to feel out a new grip. Her cheek was pressed against the cold rock, and she watched the sunrise while she climbed.

For the first time she could see the valley floor beneath her. Fingers of rock jabbed upward, and the drifts of snow looked like a dusting of powdered sugar. Terrifying as it was, it wasn't the distance below her that scared Kelly; it was the distance above. She was so tired that she knew if it was very far, she'd never make it. She looked up, and saw that her long struggle had left her only twenty feet from the top of the cliff. Twenty feet was just barely possible.

Moving slowly, Kelly pulled her feet up and onto an even-smaller ledge. She put her weight on it only gradually, and when she was sure it would hold, she lifted her left hand and searched for another, higher hold. Her fingers found a crack in the rock, and she moved her right hand up. Then she lifted her feet onto the spot where her hands had been a few minutes before, and the whole process started again.

The climb went much faster in the daylight.

206

Soon there were only ten feet of cliff above her, then five. There was a ledge there, a wide ledge on which Kelly could stand and put her hands over the cliff rim onto the blessed flat ground above her.

For most of the climb Kelly hadn't thought about what Marshall might be doing. She wouldn't let herself think that Lauren was dead. She thought about nothing but the climb. Now, with the end in sight, all the anxiety came rushing back. Kelly took a good grip and began to pull herself up.

A hand grabbed her wrist and dragged her up the cliff. Another hand took her by the hair and jerked her head back.

"Hello, little girl," Marshall said. "I didn't expect to see you again." He pulled her face close to his. Blood vessels had popped in his eye, and the blue centers were surrounded by a sea of scarlet.

Kelly tried to spit at him, but the climb had left her mouth too dry. "How did you find me?" she choked out.

He jerked his head toward the cliff face. "Saw you climbing up. Never thought you would make it, but you were sure fun to watch." He leaned forward quickly and kissed her with his split and swollen lips.

Kelly pulled away, but Marshall tightened his

207

grip on her hair. She didn't ask him to stop or to let her go. She knew it wasn't going to happen. She reached out her tired arms and clawed at his face.

She was just too exhausted. After the long climb she could barely reach up, and her fingers didn't have the strength to do any damage.

Marshall threw her to the snow-covered ground and put a boot over her throat. "You flew once, little Kelly. How about I push you off and we see how you fly this time?"

He started to laugh, but Kelly wasn't looking at him. She was looking at the unlikely figure that was coming up behind him.

Lauren was approaching at a run. Her skin was pale as milk, but she had a long pole in her good arm and she raised it as she came.

Marshall drew his foot back to deliver a kick that would send Kelly back over the cliff. "Good-bye again, little Kelly," he said.

The pole whistled as it cut through the air. It rang off the back of his head, and Marshall staggered forward. His raised boot passed over Kelly and he tumbled over the side of the cliff. He vanished without a sound.

Lauren collapsed into the snow at Kelly's side. "Are you okay?" she gasped.

"Am I okay?" Kelly said. She sat up and

looked at Lauren in wonder. "I thought you were dead!"

"So did I," Lauren said. "Marshall knocked me cold and left me back at the house. When I woke up, you were gone and he was in the house digging around in the kitchen." Lauren stopped and closed her eyes.

Kelly put her hand on her friend's shoulder. "You're not okay. Where did you spend the night?"

"In one of the sheds beside the house. There was a lot of stuff in there, blankets and this." She shook the pole.

For the first time Kelly noticed the ring near the base of the pole. "A ski pole?"

"Yeah," Lauren said. "And there's—"

A hand came over the edge of the cliff and landed an inch away from Kelly. She shouted and rolled away as Marshall's other hand reached over the edge.

Lauren stood up and raised the ski pole. She swayed on her feet, winced, and crumbled into the snow. The pole bounced out of her hand and over the cliff.

Kelly took a half step toward Lauren; then Marshall dragged his face over the rim. In another few seconds he would be back on top.

Kelly felt a coldness drop over her. It wasn't the physical coldness she had felt climbing the cliff. It was a mental coldness. She stepped toward Marshall and looked down at his bloody face. She could see the ledge where she had paused near the top of her climb—it must have saved Marshall. She raised her foot.

"You don't want to do that, Kelly," he said. "You let me up, and I won't hurt either one of you. Promise." His voice was as calm as ever.

"Good-bye, Marshall," Kelly said. She smashed her ice-crusted shoe into his face.

For just a second he held on. Then his hands slipped in the snow and his feet slid from the ledge. Slowly, but with increasing speed, he fell away. He began to scream as he fell, the pitch going up and up. There was a distant thud, and the screaming stopped. Still wrapped in her mental coldness, Kelly turned away.

She knelt next to Lauren. "Lauren?" Lauren's eyes were closed and her forehead was creased in pain. "Lauren? Lauren!" She put her head close to Lauren's face and listened to her breathing. It was fast and shallow.

Kelly looked back down the ridge. The ranger house wasn't far away. Being careful to touch her injured side and arm as little as possible, Kelly got her hands under Lauren's arms and began to drag her across the snow. "Don't worry," she whispered. "You'll be all right."

Lauren's only response was a moan.

The door to the house was open. Kelly dragged Lauren right up the icy steps and into the book-strewn front room. She wanted to collapse herself—about two weeks of solid sleep sounded right—but after all this, she couldn't let Lauren die.

She walked through the kitchen. The dead woman was gone. Kelly didn't know what Marshall had done with the body, and she didn't want to know. She went into the bedroom and pulled the blankets from the bed. Then she went back to the living room and covered Lauren.

Lauren's skin was cool and clammy. She cried out as Kelly wrapped the blanket over her, and her legs thrashed feebly. Her eyes snapped open and she looked around. "Is he gone?"

"Yes," Kelly said. "Gone for good."

Lauren shook her head. "He always comes back," she said.

"Not this time," Kelly told her. But Lauren's eyes were closed again, and Kelly wasn't sure that she'd heard.

Kelly listened to Lauren's breathing again, relieved to hear that it now sounded normal, like she was asleep.

*It shouldn't be long now. I only have to find the phone, and the police and an ambulance will be on their way,* Kelly thought. She looked around the small room and didn't see a phone. Her aching legs protested, but she got to her feet and went to look in the kitchen.

There was no phone in the kitchen, either. And no phone in the bedroom. Kelly shuffled through the house twice more, even opening drawers and closets to look inside. There was no phone in the house. Marshall must have gotten rid of it.

Kelly sat on the edge of the overturned chair and looked down at Lauren. She knew it would take hours to walk the eight or so miles that remained to reach Wall. As tired as she was, Kelly was sure she couldn't make it.

Lauren moaned in her sleep. Kelly saw sweat gleaming on her friend's forehead. Her fever was back. Kelly bit her lip and wondered what to do.

It was amazing that Lauren had made it through the night after the beating she had taken. When she had run out to help Kelly, she couldn't have been running on anything but pure adrenaline. Kelly didn't believe that Lauren could last another night without medical attention.

But there was no way to get help in time, Kelly knew. There was no phone, no car, nothing. Deliriously Kelly tried to figure out how to get to Wall. *I would settle for a snowmobile*, she thought, *or a dogsled, or . . .*

Kelly suddenly remembered what Lauren had used to hit Marshall, and just where she had gotten it from. She jumped up from the chair. "Wait here!" she told Lauren. "I'll be right back."

Lauren slept on.

It was blindingly bright outside. The brisk northern wind had swept the clouds away, and the sun reflected back from the blanket of snow. It took Kelly only a few minutes to find which of the several sheds Lauren had used for shelter. The metal door opened with a creak, and Kelly stepped into the darkness inside.

As Lauren had said, there was a stack of blankets. Beside them were boxes that contained what looked like old clothes. Leaning against the wall was another ski pole—the mate to the one Lauren had used on Marshall. There was another set of poles, and beside them were two sets of cross-country skis.

Kelly took down the skis and looked at the bindings. The skis were bright yellow, with stripes of orange across the tips. She ran her hand over the slick fiberglass surface. She couldn't remember when she'd seen anything more beautiful.

She was glad to see that they were the kind that didn't require special boots. She took a pair of skis out into the brilliant sun, then went back to get a pair of poles.

213

The poles were a bit long for her, and there was no way to adjust them. Kelly would have to make do. It took her several tries to get the bindings clamped on her snow-encrusted sneakers. Once they were on, she bent over carefully and picked up the poles.

One push and she was sliding across the surface of the snow. The skis hadn't been waxed, and Kelly could feel them sticking to the snow, but they were good enough—far better than walking. She coasted to a stop and looked off down the road. The impossible trip to town should take only a couple of hours on skis.

Kelly looked back at the house where Lauren was sleeping. She hated to leave her friend without letting her know what she was up to, but she wasn't sure that she could wake Lauren up if she tried. Besides, every minute that she spent in the house was a minute she could have been on her way to get help.

Kelly planted the poles and shoved hard. The undulating snow passed under her skis with a comforting hissing sound. She worked at getting the rhythm, pushing out and back with her skis, shoving with the poles. Kelly hadn't done as much cross-country skiing as she had downhill, but the movements were familiar and it came back to her as she went on.

Soon she was gliding over the sunlit snow,

pushing and pumping, the wind whipping through her auburn hair. Kelly's arms and legs still ached from all she had put them through. For the moment, she was able to ignore the pain.

She was several miles down the road before she realized that Lauren had kept the promise she'd made at the very start of the trip. Despite everything else that had happened, Kelly was getting to ski.

# EIGHTEEN

The skis were talking to Kelly. Over and over, with every gliding step, they said, "Sleep."

She tried to remember when she had slept last. She had been knocked unconscious in the car wreck. That had been . . . yesterday? The day before? Before that? . . .

Kelly couldn't remember before that.

Since then she had walked, and fought, and climbed a cliff. She had dragged Lauren though the snow. And she had skied. She was more than tired—she was exhausted. Even if it was only another hour to the town of Wall, Kelly no longer thought she would make it. She just didn't have another hour of effort in her.

Three times she had realized that she was standing still, just leaning on her poles. Each time it took her longer to remember what she was doing, longer to coax her aching muscles into moving.

Kelly saw something at the edge of her vision and turned her head. She gasped and twisted around, almost falling off her skis. There was nothing there, but she had been sure that Marshall was standing beside the road. She shook her head and skied on.

A minute later she saw him again, crouching among a pile of boulders. But when she looked straight at him, he disappeared. In his place was only a dark patch on the rocks.

*It's not enough I have to die out here*, she thought. *Do I have to go crazy first?*

There was another figure waiting for her in the road ahead. Kelly skied straight for it, determined to rid herself of these phantoms. In the glare of the sun and snow, it was hard to make out anything but a dark form. But this time it didn't go away.

As she drew closer, she saw that it was bigger than a man. Another few steps and she saw that it was a man on horseback—and he was coming her way.

She stopped and waited for the illusion to come to her. It moved at a trot, sending up a spray of snow, and stopped twenty feet away. The horse was large and reddish brown. It pawed the ground nervously, snorting twin jets of steam in the cold air.

Kelly squinted up at the dark figure on the horse's back. It was a man in a blue quilted jacket and heavy boots. His face was shaded by a wide-brimmed hat accented with red feathers. He took off the hat to reveal strong features and coal-black hair.

*An Indian on horseback*, thought Kelly. *At least my hallucinations are showing some imagination.*

The man on horseback looked down at her and frowned. "What are you doing with Mary's skis?" he said.

Black spots swam in Kelly's vision, and there was a roaring in her ears. Her legs went limp, and she pitched forward onto the ground. The snow felt surprisingly warm against her face.

The last thing she heard was the beat of the horse's hoofs coming closer.

There was a sharp metal smell in the air. Kelly reached out her hand, trying to find the pan. She had to turn off the stove before the ranger's house burned down.

She opened her eyes.

There was no pan, and no stove. She was in a room with beige walls and a television held on a high shelf. There were shiny metal rails along the side of her bed. Crisp white sheets were stretched over her body and legs.

Kelly tried to sit up. Every inch of her body ached, and there was a dull pain in her feet. When she tried to move her arm, she saw that an IV line connected it to a bottle of clear fluid in a rack by her bed.

She knew she was in a hospital. She didn't have any idea where the hospital was, but just knowing it was a hospital was something. She eased down on the soft pillows and relaxed.

She might not be home, but it was over. They had made it through everything, and now she and Lauren . . .

Kelly sat up and looked around the room. She found a cable dangling near the bed that had a large red button. Kelly pressed the button, and kept pressing it until a nurse came through the door.

"Well," the nurse said, "I'm glad to see you awake."

"I had a friend with me," Kelly said. "She was back at the house in the park."

"Your friend's okay. She's just down the hall."

Kelly sighed in relief. "That's good. I was afraid nobody would find her."

"Well, according to John Grass, you told him about your friend over and over."

"I don't remember telling anyone. Who's John Grass? Wait, is he an Indian?"

220

The nurse sat down in the chair beside Kelly's bed. "John's from the Sioux tribal council. He was on his way to visit one of the park rangers and found you skiing down the road in the middle of the Badlands." She stopped and shook her head. "When he called for help, John said you were almost dead. He was right. We've all been very worried about you."

"But is Lauren okay?" Kelly asked.

The door opened again and a balding man in a white lab jacket came in. "I understand our little hero's awake!" he said heartily.

"Hero?" Kelly said.

"Didn't you fight off a killer and save your friend?" he asked.

"Well . . . sort of."

"That's enough to make you a hero in my book."

The nurse patted Kelly on the arm. "Dr. Rimbach's very hard to impress," she said. "But you've managed to impress just about everyone. According to your friend, you're a hero ten times over. Oh, that reminds me." She looked up at Dr. Rimbach. "Doctor, she was just asking about her friend."

"Lauren," Kelly said, "and she saved me just as many times as I saved her."

"Right, Lauren," the nurse said. "Well, I had better get on with my rounds." She gave Kelly a

221

warm smile as she left the room.

Dr. Rimbach looked down at the clipboard in his hands. "Lauren has a compound fracture in her arm and two broken ribs. There was some internal bleeding, but she's been up and around for a day, and it looks like she's going to be fine."

"A day? How long have we been here?"

"Three days," said Dr. Rimbach.

"Three days!"

"You were a very sick young woman," he said. "Your friend was injured, but you were suffering from exposure, a concussion, and numerous small injuries." He gestured toward her feet. "You've lost some skin and a bit of your toes to frostbite."

Kelly lifted the sheet and tried to look at her feet. "How much of my toes?"

"Not much," Dr. Rimbach said. "They should heal just fine. But you're lucky we didn't have to take your feet. If you'd been out there just a few more hours, you'd have been in real trouble. And you're suffering from something else."

"What?"

Dr. Rimbach settled into the chair where the nurse had been sitting. "You've heard of people doing incredible things in emergencies—little old ladies picking up cars, mothers lifting metal girders off their kids?"

Kelly nodded.

"What you did was something like that," he said. "In taking care of yourself and your friend, you did things that you would never have been able to do normally. You've pushed your body far beyonds its limits."

"What does that mean?" she asked.

Dr. Rimbach stood. "It means you're probably going to be very weak for a few days, and you're going to discover aches in places you never knew you had. You've probably strained half the muscles in your body. We're going to want to keep you here for a while, just to make sure there aren't any other adverse effects."

"What about my family?"

"They're on their way," he said. "Your parents should be here sometime this afternoon. They would have been here sooner, but we weren't able to identify you positively until Lauren woke up."

"I guess our purses are still in the car," Kelly said.

"Last I heard, the police still hadn't found the car. Well, I'll be back to check on you shortly, but now I'd better get on with my rounds." He slammed his clipboard shut and headed for the door.

Kelly didn't want to ask the next question, but she had to know. "Have they found Marshall?"

Dr. Rimbach stopped. "No," he said quietly. "No, they haven't." He took a step back toward the bed. "But don't worry. There's a lot of ground out there, and Lauren wasn't able to tell them exactly where to look."

Kelly licked at her lips and tried to smile. "You're probably right. Can I talk to Lauren?"

"I don't see why not," he said. "But you stay here. I don't want you walking on those feet until they have more of a chance to heal. You got it?"

"Yes, Doctor."

"Fine. I'll send your friend right down." He gave her a nod and left the room.

Lauren came in a few minutes later. Her arm was supported by an enormous cast that made it stick out and forward. "Hi, Kel," she said. "I was starting to think you'd never wake up."

"So was I," Kelly said. She tried to sit up straighter. "How are you feeling?"

Lauren rolled her eyes and tapped the hard cast with her free hand. "The mummy strikes again," she said. She walked over to the chair next to Kelly's bed, tugging at the hospital gown as she sat. "You'd think they'd make these things a few inches longer."

"Gives the doctors a thrill," Kelly said. She smiled and discovered that even the muscles in her face were sore.

Lauren's eyes narrowed and she leaned close to the bed. "Kel, did you really get rid of Marshall? I figured he went over the cliff, but I wasn't sure."

"He's gone, Lauren. He took a fast trip a long, long way down."

Lauren nodded. "Remind me not to pick up any hitchhikers next time, okay?"

"I reminded you this time," Kelly said.

"Don't rub it in," Lauren said, but her eyes were bright, and for the first time in days Kelly thought that Lauren might actually laugh.

"Well, we won't have to worry about Marshall or anybody else."

"Why not?"

"Because," Kelly said, "as soon as our parents get here, they're going to kill us."

"You got that right," Lauren replied. "You should have heard my dad on the phone. He was ready to bite my head off from a thousand miles away."

"The phone!" Kelly would have slapped her forehead, but her arms seemed to weigh two tons each. "I didn't even ask to call home."

Lauren did laugh this time. "Don't worry. I think your whole family is going to be here in a couple of hours. My family's coming too. Even if you called home, there wouldn't be anybody there." She brushed her free hand across her dark hair. "You should hear everyone talking about us! I think every policeman in the country has been looking for us."

"Because of the killings?"

"Because of your note," Lauren said. "I didn't even know you left one, but somebody found the note you left back at that motel and called the FBI. There's been a big search on for us. The police must have just missed us a hundred times. They all seem kind of disappointed that we got away without them, and they all wanted to be the one that caught Evan."

"Who's Evan?" Kelly asked.

"That's Marshall's real name. Evan Bailey." Lauren shivered. "You wouldn't believe how many people he's supposed to have killed."

*I'd believe it,* Kelly thought.

"Anyway, there's supposed to be an FBI agent here to talk to us sometime today."

"Where is 'here,' anyway? I forgot to ask that, too."

"Rapid City, South Dakota. We're about thirty or forty miles from the park, I guess."

For a long moment they were both quiet; then they both started to talk at once.

"I want—"

"You—"

They stopped and laughed. "You first," Kelly said.

"What you did back there, everything you did." Lauren's voice was tight, and she had to stop to clear her throat. "I just wanted to thank you."

Kelly found the strength to lean out of the bed and hug Lauren. "You saved me," she said.

"Not like you did."

"We saved each other," Kelly said.

The door opened and the nurse leaned back in. "Sorry to break this up," she said, "but you're both going to be too tired to visit with your families if you don't get some rest."

"Okay," Lauren said. She pulled away and stood, tugging again at the thigh-length gown. "I'll see you in a little while."

"Sure," Kelly said. "And, Lauren?"

"Yeah?"

"If we take a trip next year, let's go to Florida."

Lauren's laughter echoed up the hall as she walked to her room.

Kelly leaned back and pulled the sheets up to her chin. It felt good to be clean and to sleep without having her arms tied. Even the hard hospital bed felt as soft as a feather bed. She closed her eyes and listened to the sounds of movement in the hallway.

"Hello, little girl."

Marshall leaned over her. His face was a

227

wreck that revealed bloody bones and the jagged stumps of teeth. His blue eyes shone out of dark sockets sunk into black, rotting flesh.

Kelly swung at him, and her hand struck the wall over her head. She blinked.

There was no Marshall. There was no one in the room at all. Everything was quiet except for the IV bottle swinging in its rack. And her heart pounding in her ears.

Kelly worked to control her breathing and slow her racing heart. *Marshall's gone. He's dead, and you never have to worry about him again.*

A few minutes later she got out of bed. Pulling the IV rack behind her and wincing at each step on her injured feet, Kelly pushed the chair across the room with her knees. She got it to the door and shoved it firmly under the door-knob. Then she limped back to bed.

*If the nurses want in, they can knock.*

Kelly climbed under the sheets and fell into a sound sleep.

## Sweet Goodbyes

A wonderful series of heart-rending
stories that will make you cry. Ordinary
high-school girls are suddenly forced to
cope with a life-threatening illness.
Things will never be the same again, as
each girl fights to survive...

**Please Don't Go**
**Losing David**
**Life Without Alice**
**My Sister, My Sorrow**
**Goodbye, Best Friend**
**The Dying of the Light**

All at £2.99

# Scrambled Legs
## Jahnna N. Malcolm

ROCKY: *hot tempered*
MARY BUBNIK: *worst dancer ever*
GWEN: *shortsighted and sharp-tongued*
McGEE: *softball fanatic*
ZAN: *head permanently in the clouds*

Five friends at Deerfield's Academy of Dancing. What do they have in common? Nothing – except they all hate ballet!

| | |
|---|---|
| "We Hate Ballet!" | £2.99 |
| The Battle of the Bunheads | £2.99 |
| Stupid Cupids | £2.99 |
| Who Framed Mary Bubnik? | £2.99 |
| The Lucky Stone | £2.99 |
| Save D.A.D. | £2.99 |
| The King and Us | £2.99 |
| Camp Clodhopper | £2.99 |

*By Andrew Taylor*

# SNAPSHOT

Smith has a secret - something she doesn't want Chris to find out - but Chris is determined to uncover it. How else will he be able to help her?

# DOUBLE EXPOSURE

Something is very wrong with Chris and Smith's holiday cottage. Rural tranquility is shattered by a man who'll stop at nothing to get what he wants.

# NEGATIVE IMAGE

Christ is expecting a quiet weekend, just him and Smith. But then Chris is kidnapped by animal liberation fanatics, but they've got the wrong person...

# HAIRLINE CRACKS

Sam Lydney's mother has disappeared, and it's got something to do with the nuclear power station. But to find his mother, he and Mo have to work alone.

# ORDER FORM

To order direct from the publishers, just make a list of the titles you want and fill in the form below:

Name_____

Address_____

_____

_____

Send to: Dept 6, HarperCollins Publishers Ltd, Westerhill Road, Bishopbriggs, Glasgow G64 2QT.

Please enclose a cheque or postal order to the value of the cover price, plus:

**UK & BFPO**: Add £1.00 for the first book, and 25p per copy for each addition book ordered.

**Overseas and Eire**: Add £2.95 service charge. Books will be sent by surface mail but quotes for airmail despatch will be given on request.

A 24-hour telephone ordering service is available to Visa and Access card holders:
041-772 2281